FIRE ON THE MOUNTAIN

—————— BOOK TWO ——————

THE VALLEY

RICK JOYNER

MorningStar Publications

Fire On The Mountain: Book II, The Valley
by Rick Joyner
Copyright ©2018

Distributed by MorningStar Publications, Inc.,
a division of MorningStar Fellowship Church
375 Star Light Drive, Fort Mill, SC 29715

www.mstarm.org
1-800-542-0278

Cover Design: Esther Eunjoo Jun
Book Layout: Michael R. Carter

ISBN— 978-1-60708-696-3; 1-60708-696-4

TABLE OF

CONTENTS

CHAPTER ONE

THE WARRIORS

We stood at the edge of the Valley of the Shadow of Death. It was more beautiful than a dream, but more deadly than a nightmare. This day we would enter it and begin to face our biggest fears. This day our faith would have to rise above every fear if we were going to make it through. Our reward for making it through would be to fight for the greatest cause in the biggest battle there would ever be.

"You see death, but I see life," a familiar voice said. "Those who make it through this valley will live as few ever have."

Elijah was sitting on a large rock nearby. I walked over and stood beside him. As we both stood looking over the great valley below, he began to challenge me:

"Tell me what you see."

"I see the sun rising over a beautiful valley, with great and majestic mountains in the distance," I answered.

"What do you hear?"

"I hear the creation waking up. It sounds like they are especially celebrating this new day. In a strange way their song this morning seems to reflect what I'm feeling. Could that be possible?"

"What do you think?"

"I think today we will begin to face the biggest challenges we've ever faced. Could the creation be rejoicing at this?" I asked.

"What do you feel?"

"I feel dread and fear, but also faith and expectation. I know this is the Valley of the Shadow of Death, and for all of its stunning beauty it has devoured many that tried to cross it. Today it will try to devour us. But I know we would not be here if we were not ready."

Elijah nodded as he continued to survey the scene as if in deep thought.

"What do you see?" I asked.

"I see, hear, and feel the same things you do."

"Yes, but you see more than I do. What are you looking at so intently?"

"As to your question about the creation sensing what you are about to enter, the answer is 'yes.' Their songs change whenever sojourners prepare to enter the valley. They sense that what you came here to do is for them as well, and so they rejoice. At present, the creation is more in touch with you than you are with the creation. That too will change.

"The creation is travailing for the manifestation of the new creation to retake its place over the earth and to be restored again to what it was created to be. What The King did was for the whole world, and what you are doing by following Him is for the whole world as well."

"I'm glad there's no pressure in this," I quipped. "How can anything so beautiful be so deadly?"

"Is there anything more beautiful than one who lives the life of the cross to lay down their life for The King?" Elijah replied.

"I wonder if I have ever seen such a life," I replied.

"If you wonder whether you have seen such a life, then you surely have not. Such are too bold to miss. There are many who have made sacrifices to follow The King, but true disciples take up their crosses daily. Such have been very rare on the earth, but it is being rare that makes something a treasure, and that is why such lives are such treasures to The King.

"To get through this valley you will learn what the life of the cross is, and you will have to live it. The way to get through this valley alive is to die—die to yourself."

"What makes this valley so deadly?" asked Mary, who had walked over with a few of the others who had seen us talking. "What are the dangers we'll be facing?"

"This valley contains every evil in it that the fall of man has released on the earth. It is all of the selfishness, self-seeking, self-centeredness, and greed in all of its evil and deadly manifestations. Everything in that valley will try to make you focus on yourself and do everything for yourself. Following this will lead you into its deadly traps," Elijah answered.

"Are there other special instructions, or wisdom, we need to know to make it through this valley?" asked Mark, who had also joined us.

"There is no wisdom greater than the cross. Those who walk in wisdom are those who take up their cross. The King has conquered death, and if you follow Him you will conquer the death in this valley. If you stop following Him to take any other path, this valley will devour you.

"A disciple lives to follow their master, to learn of them and to become like them. This must be your resolve if you will make it through this valley. If you live the life of the cross as He did, you will conquer death as He did.

"You do not defeat an enemy by just getting past him. You defeat fear by growing in faith. You defeat despair by growing in hope. You defeat death by growing in life. True life is only lived by those who no longer live for themselves, but for The King, and do all things for His sake and for those He gave His life for.

"This valley is here to help you find true life. The only path that will lead you through this valley is 'the path of life.' But to find that path, your goal must be greater than getting through the valley. You must resolve to seek out and destroy the enemies that are in it," Elijah continued. "And there is yet one more truth you must live to make it through this valley."

"What would that be?" several asked at once.

"You must do all that you do here with joy. The joy of The Lord is your strength, and you can only make it through this valley by His strength."

We were all stunned by the last thing Elijah said and stood for a time as we tried to process it. We knew the teachings of the cross and the life of self-sacrifice, but this valley was going to require us to live them, and we knew this would be the biggest challenge we had ever faced. This was quite overwhelming, but the thought that we were not to go through the valley just seeking to escape its traps and get by the enemies, but rather seek them to attack them, was a profound change in our whole mindset and a huge stretch for us. But then to think that we had to do this with joy was really over the top.

Finally, Charles spoke up:

"This would be a radical change of not just our strategy, but my understanding of our purpose. So the path of life is found by seeking the enemy? And then to be on the offensive and attacking? I am sure most of us were thinking we needed to do all we could to avoid the enemy, to just get through it. I thought finding the path of life was done by seeking the path of life, not fighting."

"To do His will is the path of life for everyone. This is His will for you here. This valley has a high purpose, and part of it is to prepare you for the rest of your journey to the mountain, and then to be of use to The King in the great battle to come. You must become true warriors, and no true warrior seeks to avoid the enemy. You do not want to get through this valley until the work that it is here to do in you is complete, and the work you are here to do in it is complete," Elijah declared.

"You said we must pass through this valley with joy. To seek joy in a place that is so deadly is also a very radical thought. I know you're serious, but that alone would be a major challenge," another said.

"In this valley lie your greatest fears. They are your greatest threats and your greatest challenges. That gives this place the potential to be the place of your greatest victories. You cannot have a great victory without a great battle.

"In each of the great battles you must fight there are two battles going on: the one without and the one within. The one within is to find the righteousness, peace, and joy that is His kingdom. If you win that one, you will win all of the others as well.

"The Lord created this valley, but men made it the Valley of the Shadow of Death. So He uses it to seal in His people who they are called to be—warriors that do not kill, but impart life. They do not wound, but heal. They do not oppress, but set captives free.

"This is where you will experience some of the greatest evil, and it can only be defeated with the greatest good," the prophet said as he turned to face us.

"If you face each day as you should, you will end each day with even more of the peace and joy of the kingdom. If you do that you will see even in this valley a glorious beauty. When you can no longer see the beauty in it, you will have lost your joy and somehow departed from the path."

"We have dreaded facing the evil here, and having an expectation of doing this to grow in peace and joy is certainly a change in our thinking. To look for the beauty and the good here is another. I just wanted to get all of those who are with me through this place. Now you've said we must pursue the enemy and enjoy this valley. That is really a stretch," I said. "Is this required of all who go through this valley?"

"No, it is not required of all, but just those who want to make it through," Elijah answered.

"Who would not want to make it through?" someone asked.

"You would be surprised at how many spend their lives in this valley fighting things they should have overcome long ago," Elijah replied.

"'The joy of The Lord is your strength.' The strong feed on joy every chance they get, especially when facing great challenges. Joy is to your soul what physical food is to your body," the prophet said. "Without joy the soul will get weaker until it expires."

There was another period of silence as we tried to process all of this. These truths were not new to us, but it was new to try to apply them here. We knew we would have to live them now. They could not just be a philosophy we understood, but a life we lived. To fail to do this would have the most tragic of consequences. As if hearing our thoughts, Elijah continued:

"You will need more strength every day to survive here, and then even more to stay on the path. So, your capacity for all that is true and good must grow each day. The joy of The Lord increases your capacity for His truth.

"Do not just look at the consequences for not living the truth, but look to the reward for living them. It is in this Valley of the Shadow of Death that you will learn to live like never before. If you follow The King into His death, you will also follow Him into His resurrection and sit with Him where He now sits. Then you will live as the new creation you are called to be.

"Every day here will stretch you beyond your present abilities and far beyond what you think you are capable of. Here you will learn to live as He thinks you are capable of. You must find the grace, which is the strength of The Lord. This is where you come to know that you only make it through every day by the grace of God. Here you will learn the true value of the grace of God, and you will seek it every day like you do your food, water, and the air that you breathe."

Then Elijah leapt off of the rock and turned to face the still gathering crowd. Then he started to walk among us. He would occasionally stop and look deeply into a person, and then move on, still speaking to us all.

"You must have faith to see the path, and you must have love and joy to stay on it. Fear will lead you astray, and doubt will lead you into circles. Again, it will help you to keep in mind that fear is starting to prevail over you when you lose your joy and when you can no longer see the beauty around you," the prophet added.

Elijah then turned his gaze back to something in the distance that was beyond our vision. After a few moments he looked at us again and continued:

"You abide in the kingdom by abiding in The King. Today you will begin to take the authority of His kingdom into dark places. You will stand before some of the greatest evil. You need more than just faith to prevail here. You also need boldness.

"When the apostles were threatened by the Sanhedrin they did not pray for more faith, but for boldness. Faith is necessary, but boldness is what allows you to act on your faith. To prevail here you must seize the initiative and never relinquish it.

"Initiative is faith in action, but it must be joined to wisdom. You will see wisdom through your love and joy."

Then the prophet turned and spoke directly to me, but loud enough for all to hear:

"Until today, your greatest threat in leading this group was to drift from the path and your source of living water. While in this valley your greatest danger will be great danger, not just great distractions. These can take your life and the lives of those who are with you.

"You will be safer and avoid worse dangers by staying on the path, but at times they will meet you on the path so you cannot avoid them. If they can't kill you, they will try to turn you from your course, stop you, or turn you back. They will block your path so that you cannot avoid them. So to continue you must overcome them."

"Is it possible to turn back?" I asked.

"It is," he answered. "But it would be better to die fighting here than to do that. You must not shrink back from your course. If you seek to save your life you will lose your life in a much more painful way. Such as have turned back exist, but they do not live. For those who have had the faith to make it this far, it would be better for them to perish in the valley than to exist in mediocrity and fear."

"Is there no more hope for those who turn back? Could they not try again to cross this valley?" Mary asked.

"All things are possible in The Lord, but few that shrink back recover the courage to try again. Those who have made it this far are rarely of the nature of those who turn back, but if there is anything in you that wants to quit, this valley will find it. It is better to settle in your heart now that turning back is not an option."

Elijah then turned and seemed to be looking at something far in the distance. It was obvious that he was seeing a vision, so we stood in silence. After a couple more minutes, he explained what he was seeing:

"At this time a great company is being attacked by the most deadly enemy in the valley. They are right now scattering in all directions like chaff before the wind," he declared.

"Does that mean that some are turning back?" someone asked.

"The King said that those who put their hand to the plow and then turn back are not worthy of the kingdom. There is nowhere to go back to. You cannot win a battle by retreating. You become more vulnerable to the enemy when retreating. I say to you again that it is better to settle in your heart now that retreat is not an option. Turning back is worse than any death you could suffer here.

"The energy that comes from the encouragement of advancing is a great advantage. The discouragement of retreating likewise weakens your power, while it also emboldens the enemy. Some have survived a retreat, but they have only made their course far more difficult.

"You have one direction from The Captain of the hosts –forward! You were not brought here to try to sneak through the valley, but to go into it looking for and finding the evil strongholds to attack and bring down."

There was another long pause as Elijah again looked at something happening far away. After a few minutes, William broke the silence:

"What you have said requires a basic change in our thinking for getting through this valley, but you have made the truth and wisdom of it clear. May I ask why this is called the Valley of the Shadow of Death? You are saying we will be facing real death, not just a shadow of it."

"If you are in a shadow then you are very near to what is casting it," the prophet replied. "This valley is where warriors learn to live with death as a real, continuous, and close threat. This is where you learn that to defeat death you must defeat the fear of death. To do this you must do what is written: 'die daily' and consider yourself already dead to this world. Those who are dead to this world cannot fear anything from this world. This alone can kill the ultimate source of all death—selfishness."

William continued, "I have read accounts of those who displayed courage in battle. It seems that courage came to them when they resolved that they were going to die. It was by settling this that they rose up with courage. For some their courage saved them so that they did not die. Their reckless abandon also enabled them to live far better than they would have, enabling them to prevail in life."

"To those who know The King, faith in Him is the basis of their courage. When you know that you have eternal life, the fear of death will not control you. Those who die in His fight, who die facing the enemy and not retreating, will be honored for eternity and with eternity. What may appear to be reckless abandon is rather a sober and real faith in the truth. You are called to follow a Person not just principles. The Path that will get you through this valley, and The Way of life is a Person you must follow," Elijah said as he scanned the crowd. Then he looked off again into the distance as he continued:

"To find the truly noble among men is the reason for this age. Finding those who will face evil because of their love for the truth is why The King did not take His dominion over the earth after His resurrection. He provided for a time when the greatest souls find the greatest prize that will ever be offered—the 'high calling of God in Christ.' There is a race for a crown that is before you. Those who have eyes to see and hearts to understand—those who lay down their own interests to take up His—are the ones this whole age has been for. They will be His brethren, sons and daughters of the Most High."

"How do we know if we are in this race?" someone asked.

"By being on this path," the prophet said. "Those who have made it this far on the path are seeking to live for the King and do His will. To have made it this far you have proven willing to confront the darkness of your times, and to press on to follow The King regardless of the risk. Such are the noble ones The King seeks. They are the ones this age is for."

"The world is full of the potential for death every day, and these who are with me have already left everything to follow this path. Isn't daily life in this world enough of a test?" someone asked.

"This valley is the world you live in," the prophet responded. "In this Valley of the Shadow of Death you will see the veil pulled back so that you can see the world as it really is. You will see and face the death that is close to you all the time. This is where your eyes are opened to the darkness that now controls your world.

"The immature are shielded from this knowledge by many veils over their hearts and minds. They do not realize how they are constantly spared by The Lord's grace and mercy. The younger you were, the more your parents protected you from dangers you did not see or understand. The Lord does the same, but here you must grow up. Just as Abraham had a great feast when Isaac was weaned, your Father in heaven celebrates the maturing of His children. Here you will mature.

"Here you must learn to dwell in peace even when you see your enemies as they really are. You will mature faster in this valley than in any other period of your life. Maturity is seeing the truth as it is and facing it. Here you will also see The Spirit of Truth, The Holy Spirit, The Helper, more than you have before. Being led by The Spirit is true maturity.

"The fear of death brings out an ultimate selfishness, and there is no better place than this to see it and overcome it. The fear of death is an ultimate enemy to those who live by faith. This is where it will be vanquished from your life, or your life purpose will be vanquished."

We knew all of these things. We had read them, studied them, and even preached them. However, when Elijah shared them there was a weight to them like we had not felt before. We tried to absorb all that he was saying like our lives depended on it, and this was in fact the case.

Then Elijah's eyes narrowed again as if he were looking at something far away. I watched him closely as I was now convinced he was seeing a vision. Then he looked back at me and continued, again loud enough for all to hear:

"For it to be a real test the danger must be real. You know the saying that 'the brave die only once, but a coward dies a thousand deaths'? The truth is that cowards die one continuous, long, and tortuous death. True life is noble and glorious, and lived by faith. True life is the ultimate adventure and the ultimate quest.

"Those who live by faith do not fear death. They know death is not final, but only a bridge to cross to a much more glorious life. That is what you must seek to walk in now by dying to this world. You must do it while walking through some of its most beautiful and deadly places. Now is the time for you to face and overcome the ultimate enemy. To face it with joy is overcoming."

Elijah again looked into the far distance. As I watched him, I felt a remorse that I knew he was feeling. After a few moments he turned back to me and began again:

"You will cross the bridge to eternal life in this valley. All who pass through this valley will die. Those who come out the other side have died to all but Christ, and the life that they live will be Christ living through them. These have come to abide in Him, and He in them. These are the ones who begin to live in the age to come, and by this help to build a bridge to the age to come.

"You begin to experience much true life, the most fulfilling life, by dying to yourself. It is appointed for all men to die once, so once you have died to yourself death has no power over you. Here you can go beyond believing this in your mind and start believing it in your heart. It is what you believe in your heart that you are and that you live.

"This valley is the gate to the most powerful and glorious lives. The ones who make it through this valley are the Son of David's mighty men—the warriors."

Elijah again looked over the group slowly as if he was looking into each one of us. Then he turned and walked down the path into the valley and disappeared from our view. We stood watching, trying to recount and process all that he had said.

Now we knew that we would not come out of this valley alive. We would either die physically or die to ourselves so completely that it would not be us coming out on the other side. We were worms about to enter our cocoon. If we came out the other side, we would be new creatures that no longer crawled, but soared.

CHAPTER TWO

THE WORSHIPERS

As we stood looking into the valley that Elijah had just entered, I felt that we needed to take a few minutes to restate what he had said to us and discuss how we were going to apply it.

William began by outlining the two most basic changes to our strategy for navigating through the valley. First, we were to go looking for the enemy and his strongholds to attack them. Next we must focus on maintaining the righteousness, peace, and joy of The Lord, and use the joy as a barometer of whether our hearts were staying on course.

To do this we resolved to base all of our decisions on what was the right or righteous thing to do, not on what may be expedient. As Romans says that the kingdom of God is righteousness, peace, and joy, we must maintain these to abide in His kingdom, or for our actions to result in the furtherance of His kingdom. We would know that we had drifted from our course if we started to lose our peace or joy. If we lost those, we would not make the right decisions or have the strength to do what was needed because "the joy of The Lord is our strength."

Mark brought up how out of harmony we were with the purpose and strategy of The Lord before Elijah's visit. What he brought were basic principles of the kingdom, and we were far from them in our thinking. It was humbling and sobering. We could not help but wonder how many other ways we were not in sync with The Lord as we prepared to enter the valley.

Another then recounted how Elijah had said that if we lost the joy that enabled us to see the beauty of the valley then we had drifted from abiding in The Lord. So seeing beauty in all things is a barometer of our joy. To walk in the joy that enabled us to see the beauty of this valley could have hardly been more contrary to the way we were approaching it before. External conditions should not be what determined our peace or joy, but only our position in The Lord should do this.

Mary added how our joy in all things was worship to The Lord because it was an ultimate demonstration of our trust in The Lord.

"True," Mark replied. "And faith pleases God, but there is something else that we would have missed that is critical. It is written that 'The God of Peace' will crush Satan under our feet. This indicates that walking in peace is crucial to our victory over the evil one."

"So righteousness leads to peace, and the peace leads to joy," Jen recounted. "Having joy as we go through this valley is evidence that we are still on the right path."

"Okay. If we're going to go through this valley looking for the enemy to attack his strongholds, we must change the mindset of the watchmen from just protecting us from attacks to also being scouts that are looking for targets of opportunity," William added.

"Obviously, a main purpose for our going through this valley is to make us into warriors. How can we become the warriors we're called to be if we go through such a place trying to avoid the enemy instead of attacking him and his works? What kind of Christians would we be if we just thought of how we could get through this and not think about those who come after us?" another added.

"He said that we are called to be 'the Son of David's mighty men,'" Josh said. "They were some of the most outrageously fearless warriors of all time. They did outrageous things for their king. I think we too need to be looking for ways to take outrageous leaps of faith."

"Obviously, many of the Son of David's mighty men are women," William remarked. "Some of the women we have in this group are the most fearless and bold."

"They are indeed, and they can be a terrible foe if on the other side," Elijah added, who had been listening to us unnoticed from nearby.

"I did not do well against Jezebel, and neither have many since who have faced that spirit. It is the spirit of Jezebel that is a main enemy in these times. It is that spirit that still leads the world into perversion and the worship of idols. Like all evil, it is coming to full maturity at the end of this age. It has taken over much of this world and yet is greedy for more. This is an ultimate enemy in the ultimate battle at the end. Depression and disorientation are her primary weapons, which is why you must not lose your joy."

We all knew that Elijah would not have reappeared if it was not to tell us something supremely important, so our attention was riveted on him. As he scanned the group as if looking for something, he continued:

"I came to prepare you to go through this valley. This valley is the times in which you live. The spirit of Jezebel is also behind what is called 'The Great Harlot' in the Book of Revelation. You must learn to recognize this spirit in all of its manifestations, not only to make it through this valley, but for the great battle at the end.

"This spirit of Jezebel is the maturing of the evil that began when the first woman ate the fruit of the forbidden tree. This is deception in its ultimate form. It will be the women who serve The King, who have made it through this valley to the mountain of The Lord, who will be the counter to that evil one. The original prophecy was that the woman would crush the head of the serpent, and the women have a special role in the last battle. Those who are with you will come out of this valley with a special zeal to destroy this evil influence of Jezebel. Therefore, they are important warriors in all of your battles.

"The bride of Christ that emerges at the end will be the antithesis of Jezebel. She will reveal 'the beauty of holiness,' and the love of The Lord that will draw all to worship Him. Her nature will not be to take, but to give. She will be motherhood in all of its glory. Her husband and her children will all delight in her. She is what you are called to become as you go through this valley."

"To be the warriors that you must be starts with being the worshipers you must be," said Enoch, who had joined us unnoticed. "As you have said that joy is faith demonstrated, it is also worship demonstrated. True joy is the result of a thankful heart that sees the glory of The Lord in everything.

"The cherubim Isaiah saw before the throne said repeatedly that 'the whole earth is filled with His glory.' They said this because they dwelt in the presence of The Lord. When you look at this valley, at this earth, it will seem to be filled with darkness and evil unless you abide in His presence. If you abide in His presence, you will even see this valley as full of His glory. When you emerge from this valley you will be bearers of His glory because you abide in Him.

"True worship is not trying to see The Lord, but it comes from seeing Him. King David was one of the greatest warriors in Scripture, but he was also one of the greatest worshipers. As you see from his songs, he tried to see The Lord in everything and was constantly marveling at Him and His works. It is this worship that is the heart of the warriors of The Lord. They fight because they love."

As always, Enoch's joy was infectious. He did not just teach us about worship, but he made us want to worship. Together these two prophets had turned our dread of entering the valley into such vision and purpose that he made us thankful that we got to go through it. We could hardly wait to get started facing the greatest tests we had ever faced. As I turned and scanned the group, I could see the joy and vision in every face.

"The power of the joy of the kingdom is to turn darkness into light," Enoch added. "These who are with you are called to fight in the last battle in the darkest times.

They must walk in the greatest light to prevail in that battle. They must live for and live in the righteousness, peace, and joy that is the kingdom. Only such ones are the warriors of the kingdom.

"You worship what you give your heart to. What you give your heart to is evidenced by what has most of your attention. A heart that is The Lord's is evidenced by worship of The Lord. Such a heart cannot be selfish or self-centered for such are worshiping themselves.

"You have a saying that 'There are many soldiers but not many warriors.' This valley will reveal those who live for themselves and those who live for The King. Self-centeredness will get you killed in this valley. Only a pure devotion to The King will get you through. You are about to see firsthand the consequences of a selfish life and the reward of a selfless life.

"Many who are with you do not think of themselves as warriors. Some here have even said that they are lovers, not warriors. You do not really love if you are not willing to fight for what you love. This valley is where warriors are made. True warriors are made by first learning to love.

"'Love never fails,' and love never quits. You will fail as a warrior if you are not fighting because of your love. You will quit before the danger and hardship of being a warrior if you are not fighting for what you love."

Then both of the prophets looked at me as if they expected me to respond. Because they did this all of the others looked to me as well. It caught me off guard, so I just shared what I was thinking in the light of what they had just said.

27

"I made it through this valley before, but I wonder if I was given a shortcut through this place," I said.

"I know of no shortcuts, but I know of some who made it through very fast," Elijah said. "I'm interested to know why you would think you found a shortcut."

"I'm so not dead to myself yet. I'm a very selfish person, and I still have many fears. I obviously did not overcome them when I went through this valley before," I replied.

"Both are true," Elijah responded. "No one overcomes all in this place, but all leave with a resolve to fight and to be an overcomer. You can be sure that you were not chosen to go through this valley again because you failed the first time. Those who go through this valley again are given a responsibility to lead others through. To lead The King's people in anything is a great responsibility and a great honor. You are not doing this because of failure."

"That is encouraging, but I have never felt as inadequate as I do now when leading. That is magnified because I am leading The King's people," I responded.

"That is also a reason why you were chosen to lead this group to the mountain. You are inadequate, and always will be. You were not given this assignment because of your adequacy, but because you know how inadequate you are. Because of this you will be even more prone to seek The Lord, His wisdom, His strength, and His grace," Elijah continued.

"Going through any trial will not make you perfect, but in each one you will be less and He will be more. You had the making of a warrior when you entered this valley the first time, as all do who make it this far. You don't make it through without becoming a warrior, so you are already a warrior. You have learned to thrive in the fight, but you were chosen to lead a group through this for yet another reason."

"What would that be?"

"Just as there are many soldiers, but not many warriors, there are many who lead, but not many leaders. You don't just lead, but you help others become leaders. You do this by being quick to give others responsibility. Then you let them lead, even when they fail. That is not common, but it is a requirement for those who will be leaders in The King's army. This was the leadership He Himself demonstrated with His disciples, so it is the leadership of The King and His kingdom."

"I appreciate this encouragement, but I delegated responsibility because I knew I needed the help, and often this was because I saw myself as so inadequate. I saw this more as a need," I responded.

"Your sense of inadequacy will always be with you because you are inadequate, as we all are. It is where we are inadequate that He gives us His strength so that His strength is made perfect in weakness. It is true, therefore, that this was part of your motive. Yet more than your fear of inadequacy, you were determined to do what you were called to do and to help mature those who served with you. This is how your inadequacy, your weakness, became a strength that He could use.

"We all need all the help we can get from The Lord, and He often gives it through those we are called to walk with. There are none strong enough to walk alone, much less make it through this valley alone. You did not make it through alone either. You may have started out alone, but you made it with the help of the many others you met along the way."

Elijah then turned his attention to something deep in the valley. Then he turned and looked at me with the same serious gaze that seemed to look deep inside of me. He continued:

"I am an example of the delusion and defeat one will come to if they try to walk alone. The sons of the prophets kept their distance from me because I had kept my distance from them. It was basically for this reason that I was taken from the earth before I had completed all that I had been given to do. The chariot of fire was not for a victory ride.

"Remember our talks about how both my life and Enoch's were a special message to those who will fight in the last battle? I had some great victories, but you must also learn from my failures, which were also great."

"Not to detract from that lesson," I interjected, "but you fought some of the greatest battles in the darkest of times and against overwhelming odds. You were alone when you destroyed the false prophets. You did more alone than others have done with armies," I countered.

"True, but it was because I was alone that I succumbed to the depression hurled at me by the spirit of Jezebel. No one is created to walk alone. We may all do so for periods of time, and we can accomplish some things alone, but if we do not rejoin the fellowship we are called to, we will ultimately fall."

"But you didn't fall," I protested.

"Yes I did. I fell when I let the depression take over. I started to believe more in the power of the darkness in Jezebel than in the power of The Lord to keep me," Elijah countered without any sorrow or remorse, but as a statement of fact. He continued:

"I could have destroyed the Destroyer that so devastated God's people in my time. I could have destroyed Jezebel and driven the spirit of Baal out of our land. If I had invested as much in the sons of the prophets as I should have, then we together could have cleansed the land, and then accomplished what was required to keep it clean for generations to come."

"What could you have done that would have kept it clean?" I asked.

"Jesus came to destroy the works of the devil. He then said that He was sending His disciples for the same reason that He was sent. You must not be content with a few victories, but remain in the fight until evil is destroyed. Even then the work is not finished, but you must replace the evil with good. You do this by leading the people back to the worship of The Lord, knowing Him and loving Him. If the evil is vanquished but not replaced by a true worship of God, then they will fall to the evil again, just as Israel continued to do.

"You are to seek the enemy to destroy him and his works wherever you go. Then you must fill what has been the dominion of evil with good," the prophet declared, gazing deeply into me. "The Lord does not lead you into any battle without a higher purpose than just defeating the enemy, or just training His people. The Lord will make this into the Valley of the Shadow of Life.

"You and every group that comes here are part of His plan. All who go through this valley and fight in it are here to win victories and bear fruit that remains. If you just do enough to make it through, but do not make it easier for those who come after you, then your victories will be shallow and temporary. You win this battle by not just defeating the evil strongholds, but by leaving behind strongholds of truth, righteousness, justice, and peace in their place."

"We now understand this," Mary interjected. "You have imparted new vision and purpose into us. But, I thought the purpose of this valley was to train His warriors for the great last battle on the mountain. If we change it like this, then how can it be used for that training anymore?"

"That is a good question," Elijah answered. "It would be true that this valley could no longer train The

Lord's people in warfare if you totally defeated the evil here, but even the best that go through are not capable of that. Only when The King returns in His fullness will this be fully accomplished. You are doing this to prepare the way for His coming. In all that you accomplish you are helping to build the highway. Building His highway is how you prepare the way for Him.

"Enoch and I both walked the earth in the darkest of times. His times were even darker than mine, but he did not succumb to the darkness by becoming depressed. In the darkest of times he grew in his love and joy in The Lord. The times you are entering are said to be 'like the days of Noah.' Those were the times that Enoch lived in. Learn from him! It is in the darkest places, even in this valley, that you can grow in the greatest joy!"

"There are more enemies than you now perceive," Enoch interjected. "All of the evil in creation has been cast down to this earth. Some of the most deadly evil ones you do not yet see as enemies. Here you will be enlightened so that you can see them. Yet even if you completely vanquish those you encounter here, there will be more than enough enemies for those who come after you until the end of this age to face. What you must do is set it in your heart that replacing evil with good is the ultimate purpose of every fight. No victory is complete, or will be lasting, until this is done."

"I won a victory over Jezebel's false prophets, but I did not win the victory over Jezebel, or fill the void the false prophets left because I did not restore the true worship of The Lord," Elijah repeated. "I then ran from the fight with Jezebel. I could have put an end to her when she threatened me. I had been raised up for that purpose. It took years for those who came after me to finish what I had been given to do. In those years, many were lost that would have followed The Lord if I had been obedient. Jehu did the job of destroying the evil king and Jezebel, but he did not lead the people back to The Lord. Soon the nation slid right back into the evil ways that Jezebel had introduced to them.

"For this reason, no victory in battle is complete until the worship of The Lord is restored. This is why warriors must be worshipers."

Then the prophet put his hand on my shoulder and looked at me so intently I knew he was seeking to impart something more than knowledge. Then Enoch did the same. Then they moved throughout the group, laying hands on each one. After this they walked off. I wanted to talk more and ask more questions. Finally, I just blurted out to ask if they were going with us. Elijah turned and said:

"I will be with you all the way just as I was with John the Baptist and all who pass through here. I am with all who are called to prepare the way for The Lord. What is more important is that the Lion of Judah is with you. Remember that the Lion who is in you is greater than any lion. You should get to know Him better," Elijah said with the broadest smile I'd seen on him yet.

As I watched them disappear into the valley I had a great revelation. It was like a veil being lifted so that I could understand the ministry of Elijah. Elijah is always preparing the way. He is always trying to make the crooked straight and the rough places smooth for those who are to come. This is the result of the pain he had for not finishing his job. This worked in him a greater grace. This compelled him to prepare the way for The Lord and to prepare those who follow Him. His great defeat was turned into a greater victory that would help many more than he could have helped in his own day.

By this I understood why Elijah was able to share his failures with me without remorse. He had found the grace to turn his failures into victories. This was the root of the most powerful ministry the world would know, except for that of the Son of God Himself. There is no greater ministry than to prepare the way for The Lord. That is what Elijah helped John the Baptist do, and what he was here to help us do. To walk in this we too must turn all of our defeats into victories. Little did I understand how well I was about to learn this in the days to come.

My thoughts then turned to the valley. We had to leave it a better place. We had to prepare the way for those who came after us. We had to leave it safer and easier to cross. Instead of going into it trying to avoid the enemy and escape the threats, we had to go in looking for the enemies, attacking them and destroying their works. We must be the hunters instead of the hunted. We were here to attack every evil stronghold and then turn it into a place of worship to The Lord.

I could hardly wait to get started when I turned and saw Enoch nearby looking at me. He said:

"That is what will make you warriors. That is what will make you the Son of David's mighty men."

CHAPTER THREE

THE DRAGON

The counsel of Elijah and Enoch had united us in our intent to go into it with an offensive posture, to find and attack the evil strongholds instead of trying to avoid them. Even so, there can be a big difference between having your mind changed and having your heart changed. When your heart is changed the truth becomes who you are, not just what you believe. Sermons and teachings can set us on the path to change, but they alone cannot do it. The truth must be combined with experience to be changed into life. It would take the valley to do this for us.

As we stared down the path into the Valley of the Shadow of Death, our fears came cascading back down upon us. It is sobering how truth presented and understood so clearly can become so clouded when challenged. To walk out the prophetic counsel would take much greater courage than had been required of us before.

"This valley feels like a weird house of horrors," someone said as we walked.

"To those who live by fear and not by faith, no doubt it is," Charles answered, trying to counter what we were all beginning to feel.

"'This does not represent our world—it is our world,' Jen reminded us. "Here we are going to have our spiritual eyes opened to reality. Here we will begin to see our world as it really is. I for one am looking forward to this."

"They say 'ignorance is bliss,' and it may be in this case, but I too would rather see things as they are. I may regret it later, but how can we not want to see things as they are?" Mary added.

"How do we know that things are not even better than we perceive them?" another said.

"That's an interesting thought," Mark interjected. "Why do we always expect the worst? Why not expect the best from our experience in this valley?"

"It may be best not to expect good or bad, but just resolve that regardless of what we see and come to understand, our first job is to maintain the joy of The Lord," William contributed. "He promised that He would not allow us to be tempted beyond what we could endure, so let's keep our focus on enjoying Him and each day that He gives us."

"We would not have been told to keep the joy of The Lord if it were not possible," Mark added.

"We enter His gates with thanksgiving and His courts with praise, so we must begin each day by thanking Him and determine that we are going to thank Him for all things," William continued. He was trying to be encouraging, but his voice revealed that he was as nervous as the others.

We seemed like troops about to enter combat for the first time. We had been through a lot together, but this valley represented a whole new level of challenge for everyone. Even so, as we walked it was good to see how the group tried to fortify one another. It would have been more concerning if we did not have some fear. We were walking into an ultimate reality and the first thing we needed was to be real.

I had been through the valley before, but not as a leader. I felt like I was carrying the weight of every soul. My whole focus had been to get everyone entrusted to me through the valley, and this all changed when we were told that we were entering it to find and fight the evil there. My mentality had to change from being a shepherd to being a commander who had to order his troops into battle, knowing there would be losses.

As I walked and processed this, I knew that I could not quit being a shepherd. These had become more than loved and trusted friends—we were becoming a family, even more than a family. Somehow I had to add being a commander and lead my family into battle. I began to have empathy, and maybe even envy, for pastors who always played it safe, seeking to have peaceful and tranquil congregations. How could one purposely lead those they had become so close to into battle? I was struggling.

"You could not help but to love Enoch," someone said, bringing up a subject that would surely brighten everyone's thoughts.

"He made me think of a friend I had when serving in the military," another added. "Even in the most serious crises he would crack a joke that you could not help but laugh at. It would change our perspective, and somehow imparted courage."

"Friends like that are priceless, and everyone loves them. However, with Enoch it was not levity, but a joy you could tell was based on an unshakable peace," Charles remarked.

"I think it is the result of having all that he is centered on being a consuming love for God. Being with Enoch did not make you want to laugh so much as worship and be thankful," another said.

"Those two turned what had been a terrible dread in me into something to almost look forward to," Jen continued. "I was fearing the darkness in this valley and had not considered that we could experience joy here. That certainly puts a different twist on this part of our journey."

"I guess that's why James wrote to 'count it all joy when you encounter various trials.' The bigger the trial the greater the joy should be," Mark added.

"The valley looks so beautiful from here," Jen said.

"It does look beautiful from up here," Mark replied. "Everything seems to become more beautiful the higher you view it from. We couldn't get any higher than being seated with Christ in the heavenly places, so if we stay seated with Him, anything we look at from that perspective should be beautiful. That is where we need to see all things from."

Charles, the leader of the watchmen, interjected:

"That is true, but where we will actually be walking is in a very dangerous valley. If we look at it from here it looks docile enough, but we will be facing some real dangers. I want to see clearly from this perspective on the ground too."

"Since we are both natural and spiritual beings we need the best vision from both perspectives," William added. "That is not easy to have or walk in, but I think we are about to learn how."

"Living by faith takes faith. I think we are about to be forced to grow in faith," Charles added.

"I think we have the team here to get through this valley, if we stick together. It is good to remind each other of the truth we know," William said.

Listening to them was helping me to process the conflict in my own heart. It was when I looked from the earthly, temporary perspective that my vision clouded. As I began to see my purpose to help them reach their eternal destinies, which meant daily sacrifice, and even martyrdom, the burden began to lift.

Then it seemed that the whole group turned to me as if waiting for my comment:

"Listening to all of you is encouraging. I know of no other group of people I would rather be entering this valley with than you. I'm glad you're all so upbeat. Getting through this will be much easier for all of us if we lift up one another and become the team we're called to be. Let's keep in mind that to remain a team we must think of others and not just ourselves. We must be sensitive to the weak and wounded as there will be some, and let's be ready to help those who need help. Keep in mind that selfishness is the core evil we are facing, so let's not let it use us."

"Our purpose for going through this valley has been changed, and it is much more encouraging to think of ourselves as the hunters instead of the hunted. Yet it seems that if we do that we will be in the valley much longer than we would be otherwise," another commented.

"What is more important: getting through here faster, or getting through here better?" Mark asked.

"We've been told that we are to leave the valley safer and easier for those who come after us," someone added. "If we do not do that we do not succeed."

We walked in silence for a bit until Mary spoke up:

"I thought this was supposed to be a dangerous place where all who go through it are tested and grow in faith. Why would it help them if we make it safer?"

"That's the same question I had. If we completely destroy every enemy we meet, it will still be a very dangerous and challenging place for those who come after us. It is written that Jesus came to destroy the works of the devil, and He said that as He was sent so He was sending us. It should not be our goal, or our nature, to want to just get past an enemy that threatens the path God's people must walk. It should be our nature to destroy every work of the enemy we come to," another said.

"This is a noble resolve, but it will make things a lot more complicated," Charles said.

"It could make things impossible," someone said.

"What is impossible for men is not impossible for God. We are here to learn to walk in the strength of His might. We will not do that if we are not faced with what is impossible for us," Mark interjected.

"If we have been asked to do the impossible, then we should be expecting to see great miracles," Jen said. "I think the best of all is how we have been commanded to go into this with vision and purpose to attack the enemy rather than just seeking to save our own skins.

"We should all know by now that making it through the tests of our faith is never the whole reason for the tests. Even defeating enemies is not the whole reason for the battles we are led into. It is also about who we become by going through them."

"As we mature into who we are called to be, the less it will be about us and what we gain, but rather more about the kingdom and how others benefit from what we do," William added.

"If this valley is such a domain of the enemy, we should be excited to be led through such a target rich environment," another said.

"It is great to hear you doing this," I added. "You have not only heard the instructions given to us, but you are wisely processing them and the teachings that will help us to become what we are called to be.

"I was made your leader because I have been through this valley before. I walked with some amazing people here, and now they are on the mountain fighting the good fight. I have also fought in a battle on the mountain, but even there I did not sense the kind of unity that we have here. I have never been in any group like this one.

"However, there has been a change. When I went through the valley before we did not have the mandate to seek out the enemy and attack his strongholds. Why is it different now? Is it because you are on a different level? Or is it because the times have changed?

"As much as I might be prone to think the former, I think it is the latter—the times have changed. We are getting close to the last battle. I think the church has been wandering in the wilderness just enduring until now, but we are now at our Jordan River. It is time to fight for our inheritance.

"We are no longer to avoid any evil stronghold in our Father's land. The world and all it contains belongs to The Lord, not the devil. It is now the time to fight for it. When

Israel came to the Jordan River to cross it and fight for their land, it said that the Jordan River overflowed its banks all of the days of the harvest. The Jordan River represents death, which is why it was the place where both John and Jesus baptized. Death will overflow its banks all the days of the harvest at the end of the age. This is why our preparation for the last battle requires that we pass through this Valley of the Shadow of Death."

"It has been said that courage is not the absence of fear, but the ability to control fear rather than let it control us. Of all that is being required of us now, to grow in faith, and all of the fruit of The Spirit, I think that courage is going to be crucial for anything that we are called to do from now on. I think courage is the result of love for those we fight for—The Lord and for one another," William added.

The group walked on in silence for a while. Then William continued:

"I must say 'amen' to this being our Jordan River," he began. "But I think we are ready. I have been in many groups, organizations, and clubs, but I do not even recall a family that has become as close as I feel to this group. We did not start out like this. We've gone from almost constant friction to almost none, even though we still have disagreements. It is just now that they are more civil, tempered by our care for one another. It has been the path that we have been on and all of the experiences and crises that we have been through that have bonded us together. This too will make us even closer."

"Having the remarkable guidance and teaching from Elijah and Enoch, always coming at the perfect time, has also helped to bond us. But precious jewels are made by pressure and heat over time. The longer we stay together, the more the pressure and heat will accomplish. What we are being made into takes time as well, so we should not be in a hurry to get through any situation we are led to," I added.

"I think there is one factor you are overlooking," William interjected.

"I know there is, but that is not one we should talk about yet," I replied firmly.

We walked in silence for a long time. It gave me great hope the way this group took time like this to process what we were being taught. I knew that this was very rare, and it contributed to the way they all took their places and moved into the valley so decisively. They were walking in the light, seeing clearly where to put their feet.

After a time Mark came up beside me.

"I really get it," Mark began. "We must put the interests of the kingdom and of others before our interest in just getting through this trial. This devotion to making it easier for those who come after us has turned our dread of crossing this valley into an exciting mission, but this is about more than that. This is about becoming mature warriors of The King. We are not called to be warriors for our own glory, but for His. We should never put our own interests or desires first."

"I get it too," William added. "All that Mark said is true, but it is also a brilliant strategy. This takes us off of the defensive to taking the initiative. It is far better for morale to be proactive and intentional than to be on the defensive. This one thing was like having someone flip a switch from fear to faith."

We thought that the enemy must have sensed this resolve in us as well, and we walked for the rest of the day with no attacks. We thought that this was because we were so prepared for the fight that it had made the enemy hesitant, but that was not the case. The dragon who had been fighting God's people for thousands of years was far more cunning than that. He was carefully laying the trap and using our increasing confidence in ourselves to lead us into it.

A few times there was a disturbance outside our perimeter. These seemed to indicate an imminent attack, but the group responded so resolutely that we began to believe even more that we were so strong it caused the attackers to reconsider. We all began to think that this new resolution was going to make crossing this valley much easier and faster. We might even just march straight through with no battles, sending the enemy scattering just by being there.

As the day came to a close we found a clearing adequate for a camp, and so we stopped and set up for the night. We established the watches, and then we feasted on the abundant fruit we had gathered along the way. Mark, both Marys, William, and Charles sat with me.

"This was a great day," William began. "We made it twice as far as I expected, and the fruit here is abundant. The living water is also always close. This has been a very good start."

Mary responded, "I do not think the nights here will be so peaceful."

"I concur," Mark added. "Our enemy dwells in darkness, and this is his time. We must be even more vigilant at night."

"It is good that we're keeping the watchmen so close that they are always within sight," Charles remarked. "It is good that some of the others volunteered to stand with the watches, or to sleep near them. After such an easy start I thought we could become a bit complacent, but with darkness falling, it seems that everyone is taking on the need for vigilance."

"I don't think we should become complacent here…" Mark began before a terrible noise interrupted him.

The roar tore through the night and took our breath away. It was not just loud—it seemed to embody both terrible pain and panic. It was so startling that it was hard to tell the direction it came from. Everyone was on their feet, frozen in place, facing the camp perimeter. We all expected an imminent attack.

When there was no attack after a few minutes, I began to walk through the camp to check on everyone. Then we heard a disturbance in the lower valley coming toward us. As we braced for an attack from that direction, I instructed William to go tell all of the watchmen on the other sides and the rear to keep a close watch from those directions too, thinking they might be distracted from the real attack by the clamor from the front.

Then, as I moved to the front to add people to our watches there, I saw forms coming up the path from below. As they drew closer we could see that they were people, staggering as if wounded. It turned out that they were exhausted. As they got closer I called out to them:

"Can we help you?"

They froze as if terrified by my voice, so I asked again, walking out into the path so they could see me.

"Who are you?" one of them asked.

"We are sojourners on our way to the mountain," I responded.

The group of about a dozen people then stumbled up to us. None of them seemed injured, but they were frazzled and frightened.

"What happened?" I asked.

"We were attacked," one of them began. "Our leader was captured. Many others were also captured, or worse."

"Where are they?" I inquired, "There doesn't seem to be any of you wounded."

"We scattered in all directions," another added. "I think the wounded that could still move all ran. Some were with us, but they do not seem to have made it this far yet."

"So you just left them behind?" Mary blurted out.

"We didn't mean to. I think we just lost track of them," another said.

"Take these into the camp and take care of them," I said to William.

"I will, but what are you going to do?"

"I'll take several with me and go look for the wounded."

"I'll do that. Your place is here," William said with such resolve that I stopped.

"Okay," I responded, "but as soon as these are able to move we're all going to break camp and go out to look for the wounded. We need to stay together, so when you get to the edge of calling distance, stop and wait for us to catch up so that we stay in contact."

William agreed, and then he gathered some of the stronger members of the group and some of the watchmen and started down the path. Charles went back to get the group ready to break camp and move out. I was then surprised to see one from William's group coming back.

"What's the matter?"

"There are wounded everywhere. We hardly got going when we found more than we could take care of. We need to get everyone moving as soon as we can. It's really bad."

I sent half the watchmen ahead to take positions in front of William's team. Charles already had the rest ready to go. As I looked around at the energy of the people, it helped to allay my concerns about moving out in the dark. It did not seem likely that many would have rested well anyway on that night. I wanted to help the wounded, but I also wanted to set an example that we would be proactive with every situation.

Then an unexpected problem arose. Those who had just staggered into our camp did not want to move. Some of them began to say that they were not going, and then all of them said they were not going. When I tried to persuade them of how important it was to look for the wounded, they were adamant that they were not going back out. I felt that I had no choice but to leave them, but I first asked them if they knew what had attacked them. They did not answer.

I encouraged them to set up watchmen, and they asked if we could leave some behind to watch out for them. I told them that we needed all of our people to help the wounded, and that I was not going to leave any of ours behind. At this they became outraged, and as we left we could still hear their curses and accusations.

"I think I would rather go out to face whatever attacked them than to stay with them and get infected by what's on them," one of the watchmen said to me. "Thank you for not offering to leave any of us with that group. I'm actually glad they did not want to go with us."

"I would like to have learned more about them, what attacked them, and how they had come to such a selfish state," I responded. "I didn't think anyone that self-centered could make it this far on the path."

"The fear of death can do strange and terrible things to people," the watchman offered.

"That's a good point. This should be a warning for us. Selfishness may be the biggest trap in this valley," said Jen, who had pulled up beside us.

"She's right," I said to the watchman. "We must watch for that if it starts to show up in our group. If we start becoming selfish it can be as deadly as what is attacking us from this valley. Please pass this on to all of the watchmen."

"I think that selfishness is what is trying to attack us here in the valley. It is the main spirit I sense in this place," Jen added.

"How did you sense this?" I asked.

"I started feeling selfish in small ways as we entered the valley, but it grew dramatically as this 'dirty dozen' came into our camp. I found myself guarding my stuff instead of thinking how I might share something to help them."

"I think you have illuminated something very important," I said. "Elijah warned us that selfishness is the dragon we're facing here, but it's manifesting in unexpected ways."

Then our hearts were frozen by a loud and terrible shriek from the path ahead. As we picked up the pace the clamor grew louder. It was not like anything I had heard before. As we turned a corner we beheld a scene more shocking than anything we had expected, even in this place.

CHAPTER FOUR

THE DEFEATED

Random fires illuminated the grotesque scene that stretched as far as we could see. The wounded were scattered in all directions. It had no doubt been a great battle, but it seemed that only one side had suffered casualties. Some were limping about and some were crawling about, but most were lying on the ground too badly hurt to move. Our leading watchmen were standing together a short distance away as if completely at a loss as to what to do.

As I walked toward William, the wounded nearby were screaming insults and accusations at me. Then as I looked closer, they were brandishing daggers as if they wanted to attack me with them.

"William! What is this? What is going on?" I asked.

"We tried to help them, but they won't let us get close. They think we're the enemy," he answered.

"Have they hurt any of our people?"

"Just one. Mary. She was trying to help one to sit up when he turned and slashed her arm. She's more angry than hurt."

"I have a right to be angry," Mary said from behind me. "I was just trying to help the guy. They're all like that. They're out there dying, but they want to kill anyone who tries to help them."

When I looked at the wounded, and then our watchmen, they looked like opposing enemies ready to strike each other. I motioned for our group to move further away from the wounded, so they moved into a small clearing a short distance away. As I approached them, several began to talk at once describing how the ones they had tried to help had attacked them.

"Is anyone else wounded?" I inquired.

"Just a few scratches," someone answered.

"First, we need to treat every scratch or cut immediately. There is a poison in these wounded that we do not want any of you to be infected by. Go dip it in the living water until you can't feel any more pain from the wound. Pray until you can't feel any more anger. Pray for these and forgive them. They obviously are infected with something very deadly."

As those in our group were doing this, I instructed the watchmen to stand at their posts all around them, not just to watch for what might attack out of the darkness, but also to not let any of the wounded get close to them. I then pulled our leaders aside to discuss the situation.

"The spirit that has taken over these wounded is the same evil that prevails over this valley," I began. "It is a spirit of selfishness and self-centeredness, but I've never seen it manifested like this. Its intent is to separate, divide, and wound, if not kill.

"Has anyone found out how this group was attacked and overcome by this?"

No one had. Neither did anyone have an idea of how to help those infected. I asked William to stay with our group while I took Charles, Mark, and Jen with me to see if we could talk to any of the wounded. I wanted to see if there was any way that we could help them while also understanding the attack that had done this, expecting that we too would be assaulted in the same way. We finally found a few that would talk to us even though they would not let us get close to them. What we learned was even more alarming than the scene.

They had not been attacked by any outside enemy. An argument had escalated until a fight broke out. Soon everyone in their camp was fighting with others in their camp. Now hundreds lay wounded all over the landscape. Then they said that this was only a small part of the entire group that had numbered in the thousands. Those not badly wounded had been scattered in all directions.

After talking a few of these decided to let us try to help them, so we carried them to the living water. Then I walked back to our main group. As soon as they saw me they began questioning me:

"What happened?"

"Who are these people?"

"Were you able to help any of them?"

"They are just part of what was once an obviously very large church that was trying to make it through this valley," I began.

"How large?" someone asked.

"From what I could gather it numbered more than ten thousand. The wounded are the result of a fight that broke out in their camp. All of these, and many more, were wounded by each other. This is only a small part of them. The rest scattered in all directions during and after the fight, but there is something even stranger about this," I stated.

"What's that?"

"With so many so badly wounded, I did not see any who were dead. When I asked the wounded they assured me that many had been killed, but no one could account for what happened to the dead."

"That is strange. What are we going to do?" another asked.

"We are going to move on and try to find any along the way that we can help," I said.

"Won't those we leave behind die?" Jen asked.

"That's possible, but we've done all that we can for this group," I replied. "We must move on."

"Isn't there anything else we can do?" Jen implored.

"If I knew of anything we could do to help them I would do it, but they do not trust us enough to let us help them."

"So we're just going to leave them here?"

"If we can't help them then the best thing we can do is to continue on the course that is set for us and pray that those who can help them will come along," I answered. "I don't like it either, but we must think of those who are with us. We're not helping anyone by just staying here when we can't do anything for them."

"For us to just go on and leave this many wounded people behind seems a very selfish thing to do," protested Jen, who was now within earshot of the rest of our group.

"I understand and feel terrible about this, but without having the wisdom or ability to help them, there is nothing else we can do."

"Don't you think God has us here for a reason?" she continued.

"I do, but it is obviously not to heal them."

"What other reason would He have us here for?" Mary chimed in.

"To learn a crucial lesson," I replied.

"And what would that be?"

"Selfishness kills," I said.

"Aren't we being selfish to leave them here like this?" Mary blurted out.

"I know it looks like it, and indeed it might be, but was it selfish for Jesus to step over all of those afflicted people at the Pool of Siloam just to heal one?" I replied. "He had the power to heal them all, but He only healed one. Why? Because He only did what The Father showed Him to do. That is not selfishness, but obedience. It can be selfishness to follow our own human sympathies instead of being obedient. I have not been shown anything to do for these people. Have any of you?" I asked the group.

No one replied. There was silence for a few moments. It seemed that the most excited were calming down. We said a prayer for the wounded, and asked The Lord to send those who had the wisdom and the ability to help them. Then we left.

When we had gotten to what I thought was a safe distance from the wounded, we stopped at the first clearing that seemed adequate for camp. The night was almost over, but we all needed rest, physically and emotionally.

As we gathered for breakfast a few hours later, there was a somber mood. We all battled doubts about whether we had done the right thing. The fruit and the living water began to revive us and soon we were moving down the path again.

After a couple of hours Mary came up beside me and started to ask what other things Elijah had shared with me when we had spoken alone. She had hardly finished the question when we turned a corner and Elijah was standing in the path. I was glad to see him as I did not think I had anything that would satisfy Mary's questions, so now she could ask him.

"I have a few things to share with you about this part of your journey," Elijah said as he scanned the gathering crowd.

"What can you tell us about the wounded last night?" Jen asked, thinking that what he would share with us was a rebuke for leaving them.

"There is a reason why this is one of the first tests you must pass to make it through this valley," he answered.

"So we passed a test?" someone asked.

"You did. You did the only thing that Wisdom would compel you to do in such a situation. Jesus is the Wisdom of God. When He walked the earth He healed all who came to Him for healing, but even He could not help those who were offended at Him, or did not believe in Him, so He too moved on from them. You did the same.

"You will not make it through this valley if you get bogged down trying to help those who do not want help, or who you have not been given the authority or anointing to help. Sometimes it takes even greater faith to move on and trust such into the hands of The Lord."

"What will happen to all of those wounded people?" Jen asked.

"Some will survive. Those who do will have come to their senses and realize that they had fallen to the enemy's ultimate trap."

"What is that ultimate trap?" another asked.

"To fight with each other. You will need all of your strength and energy to fight the enemy here, and you cannot afford to waste any of it fighting with each other. As soon as you begin to fight with each other, the most deadly enemy in this valley will have an open gate to attack you through. What happened to them started with arguments that were not resolved. Here, such seemingly little divisions can become deadly," Elijah answered.

"Those wounded who survive and come to their senses, what can they do then?" Jen persisted.

"Those will be able to join other groups that will be coming through. When they get healed, they will be able to help those groups avoid the same trap."

"You sound as if most will not survive," Mary said.

"Most will not," Elijah admitted. "Those who do not quickly wash their wounds in the living water and eat the fruit given to them will succumb to the poison. No one can survive here long without being bonded with others as a team. That bonding cannot happen without forgiveness and trust. This poison, the bitterness of selfishness, will blind most to the need to forgive. In the times you have entered, the inability to forgive will become increasingly deadly."

"When you were with us at the rock yesterday you seemed to be seeing something as you looked into the valley. Were you seeing what was happening with that group?" I asked.

"I was."

"Was there nothing that you could have done to prevent this?"

"I had tried to help them for a long time. I warned them how the poison and bitterness anyone carried in their heart would be magnified in this valley, and it would be deadly. They were sent many messengers from The Lord. They would not listen to the warnings that the selfishness and self-centeredness they had allowed to remain in their life would kill them here."

"What were the warnings? Do we need to hear them?" Charles begged.

"You have heard them, and you need to hear them. You need to hear them again while this experience is so fresh with you. That is why I'm here," Elijah began.

"What you witnessed last night was the fruit of years of teaching and emphasis on the things that feed selfishness and self-centeredness in people instead of the life of the cross that is the true path of life. That was a church built on seeking their own personal increase and personal prosperity more than seeking the interests of Christ and seeking first His kingdom.

"Of course they gave lip service to putting The Lord and His kingdom first, but that is not what they lived. Selfishness is the main spirit that reigns over this valley. Those who have not conquered their basic selfishness before coming here are the most vulnerable. This group was easy prey. No group that is built on that teaching and emphasis will survive in these times," Elijah lamented.

"Can you tell us more about the teachings that fed their selfishness?" Mary inquired.

"No one can make it through this valley without knowing and living the truth that if you seek to save your life you will lose it, and only if you lose your life for Christ's sake can you find it," the prophet exhorted.

"Was there not anything more we could have done for them?" Jen asked.

"No. You must want help to be helped. Many would rather die than forgive, and so they will. Many would rather die than admit they're wrong, or need help, and so they will.

"There are others from that church that you will come across in this valley that you will be able to help. They are the ones who scattered from the fight, but even after being scattered they did not try to go back, but rather find a way forward. Those can be helped. They will also be able to help you because of what they've been through," the prophet said.

"Is there anything else that we need to understand that makes a difference between those we can help and those like we saw last night that we couldn't help?" William inquired.

"It is all related to the same thing. Selfishness is the prevailing spirit that enables the spirit of death, and thereby is the 'shadow of death.' It comes in many forms, but the most selfish will tend to look for security first, not purpose, and not what they can do to help others. Many have truths of God but they are not built on the truth of the cross, and without that solid foundation even the truths of God can be distorted and used to mislead. Such will ultimately sow selfishness in the people rather than a vision of the true path, which is the life of the cross.

"Some who scattered after the battle last night went in directions they had wanted to go in for a long time, but they had stayed a part of this group out of fear of being left out. That too is selfishness—not wanting to miss out on what they can get. However, because they had the courage and vision to go in a new direction and not shrink back, there is still hope for them.

"There are some who left after the fight broke out who had every intent of making it to the mountain and fighting in the last battle with The Lord. Many of these had heard the warnings sent to this church, and they began to resist the greed and selfishness that was such a part of what was fed to this congregation. Many of these only stayed in this church out of selfless reasons, wanting to help their brothers and sisters get free. For these there is great hope.

"Most of those from this last group have either formed new groups already, or will do so. They are not wounded, and they love The Lord and His people. Some will join other groups moving through the valley. They will easily bond with them and be able to help to them. Some of these will be joining you. They need you, but you also need them."

"Is there any way that we can distinguish them from those that we might not want to join with us?" Mark asked.

"The Lord did not sow the tares among the wheat, but He said to let them grow up together with the wheat. Wheat and tares are hard to distinguish from each other until they mature. The Lord has allowed this for the training of His people. Consider that Jesus even knew who Judas was from the beginning, but He invited him into His inner circle. Judas was a part of the training that all of the disciples needed."

"So we should just take in everyone?"

"Wheat and tares are one issue. Keeping wolves out of the flock is another. Wolves try to separate the weak from the strong to devour them. Beware of all who try to bring separation and division. Beware of those who carry daggers instead of swords."

"Why that?" someone asked.

"Daggers are treacherous weapons. You cannot fight the battles of The Lord with a dagger. True disciples carry the sword of The Lord."

"Can you say more about what the daggers are?" one asked.

"They are truths, even biblical truths that are taken out of context. They may sound wise, but are deadly."

"What other horrors will we find in this valley?" one asked.

"That depends on you," Elijah answered.

"Do you mean we choose our own doom?" another said from the back.

"In a way you do. In this valley is every evil that has released death on the earth. No one faces them all, but the enemy is far smarter and experienced than any person could ever be. He will only test you with what you seem to be vulnerable to. This is usually some form of pride in your own wisdom or strength. You do not have the wisdom or power to resist or defeat the dragon. Here you must come to know The Lord as your Shepherd and learn to only follow His voice. He alone can and has defeated the dragon."

"But we have only had glimpses of Him on this journey," Mary shot back.

"You have seen Him and heard Him much more than you realized," Elijah replied.

Then, to everyone's shock, Elijah was transformed into The Lord, and then disappeared before our eyes. After a few minutes of stunned silence, Mary begged:

"What just happened? What does it mean?"

"What do you think just happened, William?" I asked, sensing that he had an important revelation.

"I think The Lord has been appearing to us all along as Elijah," William replied. "He appeared to the men on the Road to Emmaus 'in a different form,' and they did not recognize Him because they only knew Him by His appearance, not by the Spirit. I think He may do this often. That is why we must come to know His voice and discern when He is speaking, regardless of who He seeks to speak to us through. We must learn to hear The Word Himself, not just His words," he concluded.

"So it was not ever Elijah that we were meeting with?" another asked, looking at me for the answer.

"I'm not sure," I replied. "In experiences I've met a few biblical characters, but I was never sure if it was really them or just a prophetic experience. At times I learned that they were The Lord appearing to me as one of them because the person He appeared as was part of the message."

"So how are we ever going to know?" Mary Jane asked.

"Right now I think that if it mattered we would know. Regardless of who is speaking to us, whether it is people we know well, an angel, or a biblical character, we must hear the voice of The Lord in them when He is speaking to us. Those who appear to us may be part of the message, but only Jesus is The Word and The One we want to hear."

"So it is possible that it was never Elijah, then could it be that Enoch was also The Lord?" another asked.

"I really don't know. I would not jump to that conclusion either. It is a mystery. Maybe we will understand it in due time, but I think our main purpose here is to know The Lord as our Shepherd. We must focus even more on knowing Him and His voice," I added.

"The Lord did not just give us the answer—He is the Answer. We have a great advantage over the dragon—we have The Lord as our Shepherd, and we have The

Helper. They have much more than thousands of years of experience—they have eternity. They existed before time."

"Here we come to know that the Path of Life is the Spirit of Life that we must follow," Mark added.

We had hardly started through the valley and it had already been more challenging than we had ever anticipated. As I tried to gather my thoughts, I could only think of how far over my head I was trying to lead anyone through this, much less a group such as this. I knew I could not make it without knowing The Lord much better than I did, and I knew that was the point. As the coming days unfolded, the gap between what I thought I knew, and what I needed to know, would get much bigger. By this I would become insatiably desperate for the grace of God through which His wisdom and power was given.

CHAPTER FIVE

KILLING DEATH

A s we continued deeper into the valley, we were looking for enemy strongholds to attack, but we had not found any yet. This gave us needed time to digest all that we had learned from the devastation of the large church we had run into. Every night in our council meetings more revelation had come about the selfishness that was the main spirit of the valley, and how we could expect it to be a main feature of the enemy strongholds we were seeking to attack. These revelations would later save us from catastrophe.

The scattered and wounded from the large church had caused another big change of perspective. Now we had a growing devotion to helping recover and restore wounded, disoriented Christians. Each seemed to bring unique new challenges, but also priceless revelations. It was all coming at us so fast and was working in us so deeply that it was a bit overwhelming at times.

Still, we kept moving and dealing with the new challenges as they came. Continuing to take the initiative and being proactive helped. This gave us momentum and energy. Even so, Mary was the first to bring to my attention how we were being stretched so thin that our unity was being tested and many had lost their joy.

While I was discussing this with her, one of the watchmen came and reported that all of the others were at their posts, and that all was quiet, even peaceful as it had been for many days. This had caused them to be even more concerned that the enemy was up to something big.

He also reported picking up a few stragglers from the embattled group that were in better shape than those we had met since the first night. They were being ministered to and getting their wounds treated, but they were doing well except for still being very cynical and distrustful.

"That cynicism may be different from the insane rage we found in the others, but it is no less poison," Mary said. "We need to be careful to watch them, and those who are ministering to them, to be sure they do not become infected with this too."

"That's wise Mary, but you seem to have firsthand insight into this," William said. "Can you share more?"

"I have a lot of firsthand knowledge of it because I have had to fight this cynicism my whole life. I think this comes when there has been abuse by an authority figure. When this happens, especially when you are young and when it is by someone who is older and trusted, it causes a very deep and terrible fear that is really hard to get over. This makes it hard to trust anyone, especially if they are an authority," Mary said.

"So you were a victim of this?" William asked Mary directly.

"I was, and almost every young girl I know of was. We didn't talk to the boys about this type of thing, but I know many of them were too," she answered.

I asked Mary if she would be willing to go to those who were trying to minister to the wounded and share with them anything that may help them better understand what they were dealing with. I also asked her to try to find out specifically if there was this kind of abuse in that large church that was destroyed. Knowing the source of their division could not only help us to help them, but also help us to protect our own people.

"I'll be happy to, but why would you want me to since I too have been a victim of this and still have my own wounds?" Mary asked.

"I trust you because whatever you suffered did not steal your honor. You are an honest person and a very bold one. You're not afraid to speak your mind. You seem well down the road to being healed of your wounds," I replied.

"I sure don't feel healed. I still have a lot of bitterness toward those who abused me. Please tell me more about why you think I'm getting healed of this," she asked.

"God does not wound us, but He obviously allows it or it could not happen. Since He allowed it we know that there is a purpose for it. There is a high purpose in every injustice allowed to afflict His people, just as there was a high purpose in the greatest injustice there will ever be—the cross. Through that injustice, salvation and healing has come to the world.

"It says that through Christ's stripes we are healed. By the wounds He suffered so unjustly, He received authority for healing. The same is true with us. For those who are wounded, once healed they can be the most effective in healing others. I think you are going to have a special gift for healing these wounded ones, and you will also find the rest of your healing by being used to heal others."

"I don't know if I completely trust you as our leader yet, but what you're saying seems right to me. I do have a deep desire to help these wounded ones. This pain has dogged me for so long and cost me so much in life that I want to be as completely free of it as I can, and I want them free," Mary said as she turned to go.

"What a remarkable young lady," William said. "I can't understand how someone like her has remained single for so long, why some prince has not found her yet."

"I think they have, maybe even a few have, but she pushed them away," I responded. "However, I think that if she makes it through this valley she will not do this to the next prince. I think she is going to find her healing here, as the rest of us are too."

"Do you think that someone like me could ever attract someone like her?" William added, smiling broadly.

"William, I have never tried to be matchmaker because I think I would be the world's worst. I am always shocked at the marriages that work and at the ones that don't. Even Solomon said one of the great mysteries was the ways of a man with a maid, and I long ago gave up trying to figure it out. So, all of that to say that I also stopped doubting the possibility of great marriages happening with the most unlikely of pairs," I responded.

"You're very generous, but I know she's far too young and beautiful for me," William sighed.

"William, you're older in years but young at heart. She's young in years, but old in her heart. You may be closer than you think," I added.

"So you really think it's possible?"

"It is possible, and it may be perfect. I'm not saying that it is, but I have learned not to count out almost anything in human relationships. People are diverse, and so are relationships. In human relationships, one plus one does not make two, but they have an almost infinite possibility for increase when they work. They are truly one of the most fascinating things to behold in life."

I was not trying to encourage William in anything with Mary, but as I watched him pondering these things, I knew that I had. I did not know if it was a good or bad thing. Mark walked up at that time and gave a perfect opportunity to change the conversation.

"Mark, what insights do you have for us from the recent events?" I asked.

"I'm still digesting the lessons we should learn from the battle that the large church fell into. I just don't understand how they could fight with each other like that, especially in this place where there are already so many enemies trying to kill us," he answered.

"It seems that we are facing an enemy that logic does not apply to. It was the primary enemy in this valley that got into their camp and started that battle. It does not seem that they were prepared for it at all," William said.

"How could it happen so fast? They had just entered the valley," Mark continued.

"They had gates of hell that were wide open into their camp," Charles interjected, having walked up in time to hear the conversation.

"What do you mean?" Mark asked.

"Gates of hell are doorways through which the devil gains access to us. If we have areas of our life open to the devil, he also seems most patient to wait and enter through them at the most devastating time. I guess theirs were so open he did not have to wait long. We can all be selfish, but if it is a major stronghold in our life, that is a very dangerous place," Charles added.

"Charles is right," William said. "This is a conversation that we need to have with the whole group, but something important has just occurred to me. We've been wondering why our journey since the first night has been so quiet and peaceful. We've been thinking that this might be a precursor to a really big attack, but I think we may be looking in the wrong place for it to come. I don't think it is going to come from without, but from within."

"Or both," Charles added.

"I don't think the attack on us will be like the one on the large group," Mark said. "We've been under a lot of stress here, but we're too close for something like that."

"I also don't think we have been subjected to the abuse of authoritarian control the way they were," William added.

"That is not the only gate of hell," I replied.

"Charles, please gather the watchmen that are posted to walk throughout the camp and bring them to me immediately," William ordered. "Ask Mary to join us as well."

As the group came together we discussed how the big attack on us could come from within rather than from outside. I then asked for any observations from those present that could be an indicator of how or where it could come from. Several responded that they had noticed some starting to make much of little disputes or irritations. Others expressed being homesick, feeling lonely, etc., indicating that they were starting to look back in their hearts.

We discussed ways to combat the exaggeration of offense and growing fear. It was an insightful interchange, but it also caused me to feel uncomfortable. It could be dangerous to be too introspective, or too prone to look for things in others, especially when there was already a tendency to exaggerate problems. It seemed like there was something else we were not seeing. This proved to be the case, and it surfaced quickly.

The attack began when a group of stragglers wandered into our camp wanting to join us. They seemed in fairly good shape with no apparent wounds, so we took them in. No one seemed to suspect that they would become the source of the worst attack we had yet faced on our journey.

After just a few days, these stragglers had sown many doubts about our strategy of seeking to find and destroy the works of the enemy. They shared stories they'd heard of the doom of those who had done this. Then they began to sow more doubts about the general direction we were headed. Next they began to belittle the leadership in subtle ways. In a short time they were second-guessing almost every decision the leadership made.

When Charles recommended a certain course, they said that it was a path that none had made it through before because of the fierce enemies in that part of the valley. Then they claimed to know a much better and safer course to take. When I saw the whole group inclined to take the safe course I knew something had gone awry. We had resolved to go through the valley looking for the enemy, not avoiding him. A change had obviously taken place.

One morning I was very surprised by how some were challenging the plan for the day. Then some began to challenge our general course and our whole strategy with uncharacteristic venom. We were used to challenges and people speaking their mind, but this had a much more serious and sinister tone to it. I was considering how to address it when Mary II spoke up:

"I sense a fear and discord in you that I have not felt before. Where did this come from? It is foolish to abandon a plan before it has been proven wrong, especially for another direction that is actually no plan or strategy at all."

"I felt the spirit of the enemy more than the Spirit of The Lord coming through this doubt and fear," another added.

It was encouraging the way these had spoken up, and I was about to address the whole issue when a terrible screeching noise came from the perimeter. It was followed by loud screams. As we rushed to the place of the clamor, the same started to come from two other directions. Everyone in the camp then moved as fast as they could to the perimeter to confront whatever it was.

Charles ran up to tell me that some of our people from where the first sounds had come from were seriously wounded, but no one was able to describe what attacked them.

"Most of the others are standing their ground, facing whatever it may be, but we don't know what it is," Charles explained.

I told Charles and William to make their rounds to get the wounded help and to encourage the others to stand. As I got to the perimeter, everyone had their shields and swords drawn and ready. Then a great clamor arose from the other side of the camp. When I finally got to the point where it was coming from, I found more of a celebration than a battle.

"What happened?" I asked.

"Terrible creatures came into the clearing and started threatening us, so we attacked them. I don't think I have ever seen such fear on a creature before. They fled and we chased them until they disappeared," replied a smiling young man. "We would have gone further, but we knew we shouldn't lose contact with the group."

"What is your name?" I asked.

"Adam."

"I don't remember seeing you before," I said.

"I joined your group a few nights ago. I was with some others. We were from a large church that was seeking to go through this valley, but we were scattered," he replied.

"We came upon the battlefield and saw the devastation. I'm very sorry," I said. "I'm sorry that we could not help your group more."

"Thank you. I am still a bit in shock from what happened to us, and how fast it happened. We were a very large force, and we thought we were invincible. I'm thankful to have found this group and to be accepted by you. Your resolve to fight gave me hope again."

"You should have seen him fight," Jen said. "He was a bit slow getting started, but when he did it was something to see."

"Thank you for jumping in and helping," I continued. "Where are the rest who joined us from your group?"

"I'm not sure."

"They left," William answered. "I saw them slip away when the first sounds of this attack were heard. I tried to stop them but they fled."

"My apologies sir," Adam offered. "I'm actually not surprised."

"Why?" William asked.

"They have always been distrustful of authority. They could hide in the large group, but not here. They tended to sow their distrust in others every chance they got, and it began to affect your people here pretty fast," Adam lamented.

"So that was the source of what was starting to surface in our group? You don't seem like that at all. Why would you be with such as those others?" William continued.

"One of them was my brother."

"Then why didn't you go with them?" I asked.

"I really did not know they would desert us like that, but I would not have gone with them even if I had known. It wasn't right. It was here that I began to see that our whole attitude was not right. In the time we've had here—and watching what they were doing to your people—I wondered if we had not been a major cause of what happened to the church we had been a part of. I had already resolved that I was going to stay away from them if I could not persuade them to stop what they were doing," Adam offered.

"Adam, I'm sorry, but don't give up on them. If they made it this far they have a lot going for them, and we'll be on the lookout for them," I said.

"Thanks, but for your sake, you don't want them in this fellowship. They will tear you apart if they can. They started trying as soon as they got here. You've just started to witness the kind of discord they can cause. I'm sorry that I did not warn you about them before now. I'm sorry that I did not try to counter their poison."

"Adam, you're a remarkable young man, and we're glad to have you," William said, which the others affirmed.

There was a lot to do to take care of the wounded, and I felt that by the time we got ready to move out the day would be gone. So, we decided to camp for the night. We used the extra time to gather some of the team around to process all that had just happened.

We had been attacked from within and without in an obviously coordinated way, but we had successfully resisted both. We had some wounded, but they would recover. We considered it a victory, but later we would learn what had been accomplished that day in the battle.

We had been brought to the point of division from within and been attacked from without at a time of serious weakness, yet we pulled together and fought together. Unity among God's people is what hell fears the most, and the end result of this attack on us was greater unity in our ranks. This had sent shockwaves through the camp of the enemy, and they now suffered the kind of discord and division they had sought to bring on us.

Unity is easier, but it can be superficial in times of peace and prosperity. When our unity is attacked, its true state is revealed. Even though we had done well, we could have done much better. We did not understand the significance of this victory, and we were not ready to take advantage of it to attack a weakened enemy. We had been in a position to bring about a truly great victory in the valley, but we failed to do so.

We still did not have the vision or understanding of what was really going on, but we would get a great deal more insight through what was about to unfold. You don't have to understand everything about electricity to turn the lights on. We may not have discerned everything that was taking place in the spirit of the valley, but by just doing what we thought was right, a cascading series of events began throughout the enemy's domain.

CHAPTER SIX

THE COUNCIL

The leaders gathered in a small circle. A few paces away some of the others gathered to observe. Adam sat close by as well, intent on learning more about our ways. I began with a short overview of the events we had experienced in the valley and invited the others to comment on what they had learned from them. I was not surprised that Mary was the first to speak as she tended to be so engaged and in-touch with what was going on:

> "The infighting that destroyed the large group we ran into seems to have been caused by a buildup of unhealed spiritual wounds. These were caused by things as petty as disappointment, but when combined with the frustration of a controlling elitist leadership that the people had been losing trust in, it became toxic and volatile. These were like noxious fumes in the spiritual atmosphere of the whole group. When there was a spark, maybe even something seemingly very small, it ignited the night they started fighting each other."

"That is what you concluded from talking to the wounded and the stragglers?" she was asked.

"Yes, it is. That's the simple, basic answer. Some of the survivors we took in from that group were still inflamed from the conflict and brought their bitterness with them. They tried to affect our people. The attack we experienced on the perimeter seemed to be coordinated with the attempts from within to divide us. We were strong enough this time to survive this, but we were wounded by it, and some of our people will take time to recover."

"I would like to add that we prevailed against these attacks at least partly because of Adam's brilliant fighting skills," Charles stated. "This young man had been a part of the group that was seeking to sow discord in our camp, but he became one of our greatest defenders."

"The rest of that group deserted us when the fighting began. That is usually the case with disgruntled people, but I agree that Adam's heart and skills in the battle made up for any damage this group may have caused. He is an inspiration to us, and we owe him our gratitude," William stated.

I watched Adam shifting uncomfortably as we thanked him for what he did for us in the battle. We asked if he had anything to say. He was shy and it seemed to take as much courage for him to speak as it did for the battle, but he gathered himself and began:

"First, I want to thank you for taking us in and being willing to let us be a part of your company," he began. "I'm sorry for the way we treated you after this kindness, seeking to sow discord and undermine your leadership. It was wrong. I can see that we judged your leadership to be like that of the fellowship we had come from. I don't know your leaders very well, but already it seems to me that they are different, and you as a fellowship are different. Just having a dialog like this is something we never had, or even considered possible.

"I'm also sorry that the rest of my friends deserted when the battle began. They may be disgruntled and rebellious, but I did not think they were cowards, and I'm sorry for it."

"What made you stay and fight with us?" Mark asked.

"Regardless of whether we agree on everything, we are all brothers and sisters in Christ, and you were under attack. It never occurred to me to do anything else but fight with you against it," Adam replied.

"Adam, we are glad that you are with us. I think I speak for everyone when I say that you are forgiven for any intent to bring division into our camp," I responded. "I for one have been guilty of the same thing, and I suspect that most of us here have as well. That is in the past, and now we must focus on the future. We are glad to have you with us.

"It is likely that those you came with will contact you. If they do, please try to persuade them to meet with us. They will not make it through this valley alone. If they could see that they also need us, maybe we can help each other," I continued.

At this several in leadership and several of the observers became noticeably uncomfortable. Then several asked why we would do this, seeing that they were here with evil intent and had deserted us in the battle. I responded:

"I understand your concerns, and I do think we will have to be cautious with them. However, which of us has not been disappointed, let down, or hurt by leaders or fellowships we were a part of in the past? We have gotten over it to join together in this fellowship. We who have found this grace must always be ready to give it to others," I began.

"But they deserted us as soon as the fight began," Mary protested. "They are unreliable. They may have reasons for not trusting leadership, but we have reasons for not trusting them."

"I do not intend to trust them until they earn our trust, but I think we must always be ready to give those who failed another chance. How many chances has The Lord given to each of us? But that is not my only reason for being open to taking them back."

"Your grace toward those who fail is noble, but it also may be misplaced," Mary II added. "In this case, it seems to not only be unwise, but also dangerous for the rest of the group. What reason do you have that could be so important as to put our whole group at risk?"

"There is no doubt that risk is involved, but I would never put any of you at risk if I did not think that the risk of not doing something could be even greater. Remember how Elijah and Enoch told us that we would need many of the stragglers we pick up in this valley to make it through? Several times in my life the ones I disliked or distrusted the most became the greatest blessings. I think those deserters could be essential for us. Please bear with me as I explain.

"Consider the Apostle Peter. He denied The Lord three times, but The Lord never gave up on him. Just a few weeks later, Peter seized leadership on The Day of Pentecost, resulting in thousands of salvations. As the Apostle Paul explained, it is the grace of The Lord that His strength is made perfect in weakness.

"The Lord also said that those who are forgiven more tend to love more. Are we going to give up on a brother or sister in Christ after one failure? How about two? How about fifty? What is the limit that The Lord gave us? What is the limitation of the power of the cross?

"By the end of this journey, I think we all will have had to forgive each other many times. Some will be heroes one day and goats the next, just like Peter was throughout his life. He was commended by The Lord for hearing straight from The Father, and then he was called 'Satan' by Jesus seemingly just a few minutes later. Even so, it was Peter who was given the keys to the kingdom. The Lord never took them away from Peter, even after his many failures.

"My point is that grace, mercy, and forgiveness is the foundation of our faith. We must not abandon these foundations in this place, or any place, without disconnecting from the purpose we fight for."

After a long, uncomfortable silence, William spoke:

"You have a point, but I'm still leery of bringing back into our camp those who came in with the intent of bringing division and then deserted us at the first attack when we needed them the most. There are failures that are more serious than others, and we must treat that like the toxin they are."

"Your concern is justified," I responded. "We should remain wary of them and vigilant until they have earned our trust. However, I think our default should be that we will never abandon anyone just because they have a failure, or many of them. We must not limit the power of the cross to redeem and save, but neither does this mean that we should trust anyone before they have earned it. If those fellows show sincere repentance, their weakness may also become a strength. They could end up having what we need to accomplish our purpose here and make it to the mountain."

Then Adam spoke up:

"I've been very wrong about a lot of things, but I don't think I've realized how wrong I've been about one thing until now. My brother is with those deserters, and I was led to The Lord by one of them. But I was so angry and disappointed at them for deserting us that I didn't want to see any of them again. I know now that to be that way is to desert them, and I don't think it is the nature of our Savior to desert people. I agree that they need to earn your trust, but I pray for the grace to never desert anyone that The Lord gave His life for."

There was another long silence, then more discussion followed. It was one of those cases where it would be hard to disagree with any of the comments or either of the positions. Even so, it seemed that a turn had gradually been made, and most now agreed that it was the right thing to do to give the deserters another chance. Finally, William put the consensus into words:

"To follow The Savior, we need to have forgiveness as our default. This is something we must maintain, but here I see this as a key factor to victory over the spirit that reigns over this valley. We may pay a price for our generosity, but it is the right thing to do. I don't think we should deny anyone the opportunity of another chance. However, that does not mean that we let our guard down with them. That is a simple but honorable policy."

We then spent time evaluating how the unhealed wounds were the gate of hell that the enemy had used to attack us, and how he had coordinated attacks from without to exploit our growing division in the camp. It was a sobering but needful discussion. Even so, we were all exhausted, so I closed the discussion by asking them to bring any additional insights they had on these things to the next meeting. Then we prayed and went to find a place to sleep.

As we were departing the council, Adam asked to speak to me. He wanted to personally apologize for his rebellion. I appreciated this and told him how excited we all felt to have such a one join us. Surprisingly, he asked if he could sleep near to me.

"Of course, but why would you want to do that?" I asked.

"It's just that I was spiritually raised not to trust those in authority, but I am starting to trust you and it feels very right. Now I want to do all I can to protect you if there is another battle," he answered.

"So you're volunteering to be my bodyguard?" I asked.

"It's strange, but just a few hours ago I would have been happy to see something bad happen to you. Now I feel compelled to do all I can to see that this does not happen to you," Adam offered.

"You're a remarkable young man, Adam. I want to be sure you're protected as well and able to grow into all you've been called to be. Let's agree to watch out for each other."

We found a spot and I hardly remembered laying down. My sleep was so deep that it seemed like just a minute later that I woke with a start as William was shaking me.

"What is it?"

"We need to change the watches. I know it's only been two hours, but I think we need to go to two hour shifts, everyone is so exhausted," he said.

"I'm good with that. Good thinking. Do you need for me to do it?"

"No," William said. "I'll take care of it."

"Aren't you exhausted too?" I asked.

"I should be but I'm strangely energized," he replied. "I don't think I could sleep if I laid down, so I'll stay up with this next watch, and then I may call on you."

"Thanks," I said.

In what seemed to be just a few minutes later, William came and shook me awake again.

"Sorry, but you need to get up and come with me," he said.

"What is it?"

"You won't believe it, but this is something you need to handle."

When we got to the front of the camp I could see by the moonlight a small group of people standing. I could hear Charles talking to them. As I got closer I could see that the men were the deserters who had returned. As I walked up, Charles explained that they were asking if they could rejoin us, and that they had some very important information.

"Why do you want to rejoin us?" I asked.

"From what we've seen, we know that we cannot make it through this valley alone. Your group seems to be the strongest and most organized that we've met," one replied.

"Why should we trust you after you tried to bring division into our camp, and then deserted us when the battle broke out?" I countered.

"You're right and have every reason not to trust us," another added, seeming a bit surprised that we knew how they had tried to bring division into our camp. After a pause, he continued: "We were wrong to do what we did, and we could not blame you for turning us away. We're asking for mercy."

"Explain to me a little more how this change of heart came," I replied.

"We felt guilty after deserting you. After we stopped, we began to talk about it. Then we started coming across more dead and wounded Christians and saw how

The Lord's people are being devastated here. Those who were being picked off were the ones that were alone or adrift in small groups with no leadership or plan. We knew that we were in danger of suffering the same fate because we had no leadership or plan. We talked about it and felt that our only option was to ask you for another chance."

"So you want to join us to save your own skin, but you don't seem to have considered how you might help us?" I inquired.

"You're right. We really have just been thinking of ourselves, but I do think we can be of help. I think we are ready to change," the seeming leader of the leaderless group replied.

"I have been expecting you to return, and we have already agreed to give you another chance," I answered, noticing for the first time that Adam was standing next to me. "However, we will not tolerate you trying to incite rebellion or discord. We have too great of a threat attacking us from without to have to deal with such attacks from within again.

"Everyone in the camp knows what you did and will be very wary of you until you have earned our trust. This is not to punish you or make you feel uncomfortable, but it is a reality you'll have to accept.

"I for one can say that I very much want to trust you. I've made the same kind of mistakes in the past and The Lord had mercy on me. I think He wants to have mercy on you as well, but selfishness is the main enemy we are fighting here. You won't make it through this valley by just thinking of yourselves," I added.

"We will do our best not to cause you anymore problems. We want to be helpful. We know we don't deserve this, but we will do all we can to make you glad you have done this for us."

"That's appreciated, but again, you can expect everyone in the camp to be skeptical and watchful of you until you have earned their trust. I don't expect you to be perfect, as none of us are, but I think everyone will be especially sensitive to any bad behavior on your part for a while."

"I know that you probably have many reasons not to trust leadership, but to make it through this place, and to be an effective part of the force on the mountain, we must have strong, decisive leadership. That leadership may have flaws, but it is the one that The Lord has given us. So, if we are going to follow Him, we must also follow them," Charles added.

I couldn't help but look at William, and he was looking at me with a knowing smile. We both knew that it was just a short time before that Charles would have fit right in with this group and would have fueled their rebellion. Now that he had been given leadership, it had profoundly changed him.

One of the deserters continued:

"Until we saw the devastation we witnessed after leaving you, we probably could not have seen how terrible our rebellion was, but now we do," the one who looked like Adam replied. "I think we have all had a revelation that any leadership, even poor leadership, is better than no leadership. We will do our best to be a support to you and not be a burden."

"You must be Adam's brother," I said. "Adam was one of the heroes of the battle today. It is our hope that all of you will prove to be as honorable and courageous as he is. It may take us a while to trust you, but we want to, and we want to see you all make it to the mountain as well. We're going to need everyone we can get for the final battle."

I then instructed that they be shown a place to sleep, and that I wanted to meet with them again in the morning before we moved out. I asked that William, Mark, Charles, and Mary join us for that meeting. I then went up to each one to shake their hand and welcome them. William and Charles did the same. The group seemed genuinely appreciative to be given another chance.

The next morning we rose to a brilliant sky and refreshed people ready to go. Charles, Adam, and I had been up for about an hour briefing the former deserters about our strategy and our organization. They seemed not only accepting, but enthusiastic about it. I was starting to believe that their repentance had been sincere. I could also see potential leadership in them. It has always amazed me how so many people spend time being against what they are called to be.

As the people gathered for the morning briefing, they were obviously surprised to see the deserters with Charles, Adam, and me. Just as I was beginning my explanation, Adam's brother, Michael, beat me to it:

"We want to apologize to all of you for the way we deserted you when you needed us, and for the way we tried to sow discord in your group. We really are sorry for this and realize how wrong this was. We will do our best to never do anything like that again."

"What brought you to this realization?" Mary Jane asked.

"It was the grace of The Lord," Michael continued. "When we left you we started running into many Christians who had been casualties of this place. Those that were so devastated were like us, skeptical of leadership and organization. We soon realized that to make it through this valley, we needed the very things we had been undermining in you and in our previous fellowship. We also realized that if we were going to make it we needed to swallow our pride and ask you to take us back in. Your leaders graciously accepted us back, with conditions of course."

The whole group seemed good with this and was ready to get moving. I briefly recounted the day's marching orders, a reminder for everyone to stay in contact with the main body and for the watchmen to not just look for threats, but also targets of opportunity. Then we started down the path. As I moved throughout the group to take their spiritual temperature, I felt that there was a new level of energy and vision. Grace truly is empowering.

By midday we had not encountered any threats or enemy strongholds to attack. Neither had we come across any more stragglers or wounded sojourners. I asked Michael if they had followed the same path that we had found many wounded along. He asserted that they had, and he had no idea where they could have gone as there were so many.

I called for a quick council with Mary, Jen, Charles, William, and Mark.

"Does anyone have an idea of where all the stragglers and wounded that Michael and his group saw along this path last night could have gone?" I began. "According to them, there were great numbers in all directions."

"It's also curious that there have been virtually no signs of the enemy anywhere close to us today," Jen added.

"This feels wrong," Mark said. "I don't think other groups could have come through here that would have picked them up. We would have surely seen them pass."

"Is there any way that the enemy could have carried them off?" Charles asked.

"I don't think we can continue on until we find out what happened to them," Mary said.

We agreed and decided to set up camp and set watches. Then we formed scouting parties to go out and reconnoiter the area to see if we could find the fallen and scattered sojourners. It would not take us long to find them, and it was something that none of us had expected, or would have ever wanted to see. Now the real battle would begin.

CHAPTER SEVEN

THE REWARD

"Parallel to our path and not far away, a huge multitude is forming into what looks like an army," Charles reported. "It looks to be made up of the stragglers and wounded sojourners, but they are now being led by demons and dark princes that they do not seem to recognize as evil. They are just submitting to them."

"I've seen this army before," I replied. "What else can you tell me about it?"

"We found it by following those we saw gathering the wounded. We thought at first that they were taking them somewhere to be helped and started to hail them, but we immediately felt that something was wrong. We decided to stay hidden and observe them. I'm glad we did," Charles continued.

"I'm glad we did too," Adam said. "What they led us to was something more evil than I ever imagined.

Finding this was like seeing something out of the bowels of hell itself."

"I called it 'The Hordes of Hell.' This is from hell. What you saw is part of the devil's army that is being mobilized to attack the mountain. I have seen this army and have fought against it on the mountain, but I never knew where they got so many fallen or deceived Christians for it. Now it makes perfect sense that this is the place."

As I looked around, virtually everyone who was not on watch or with the scouts was standing nearby and listening. There was a soberness and a sense that this was the ultimate evil and danger we had encountered.

"What can we do?" Charles asked. "We can't attack them. They outnumber us many times over."

"Not to mention that we would be attacking our own brothers and sisters who have been wounded and fallen," Mary added.

"The numbers in this evil horde are far greater than what you saw," I explained. "I'm sure that what you saw was just a small part of it. It must stretch all the way to the mountain. You're right, we can't attack it yet. But what we can do is recover the stragglers and heal the wounded before they can be captured and made a part of the Evil One's army."

"How do we do that?" Michael asked.

"You may be an answer to that," I replied.

"How so?"

"You were just about to be captured by that horde before you turned back and asked to rejoin us. Can you and the rest of your group take some of our people and go out to see if you can find and persuade any wounded or stragglers to come to us?" I asked.

"Yes, but why would you trust us to do this? We were as deceived as they were until we came to our senses," Michael rejoined.

"That's why," I answered. "You know better than most what was deceiving you and what caused you to come to your senses. You know how they think, and you know what might persuade them. Can you do it?"

"We will do our best," Michael asserted.

Michael and his group seemed to appreciate being given the mission and the trust, but they also seemed concerned about such a risky task. I asked for volunteers to go with them and they soon had all they needed. Then we kneeled and prayed for the teams that were going out. I was surprised to see tears in the eyes of some of the former deserters. They were getting delivered of their rebellion just by being trusted. They would be even more healed as The Lord worked through them to be healers and rescuers. As they moved out and disappeared through the trees, Mary stepped close to say something to me that she did not want to be heard by the others:

"Are you sure that was the right thing to do, sending that group out to lead such an important mission?" she began.

"No, I'm not sure, but it seemed right. I have doubts about it too, but when I saw their reaction to being trusted with this, my confidence grew that it was the right thing to do. We'll know soon enough," I replied.

"It was bold. It would have been bold to just send them with our people, but to make them the leaders was indeed very bold," Mary added.

"Mary, there was a time when I was as rebellious and cynical as they are, maybe more so. It all changed when I was given the leadership of a small group. Until you've carried the weight of leadership, it is hard to understand it and not wrongly judge it. It was only when I was put in a position of leadership that I started seeing it correctly. I also saw how terrible and destructive my rebellion and cynicism was. The King had mercy on me, and I must have mercy on them. This may be the only way they get healed, and if they do they could be great in the service of The King," I explained.

"I hope you're right. Actually, I think you are right. That is what has been going on with me too since you asked me to take the lead helping the wounded. I think

I am getting healed of more than they are. You may have done the best thing that could have been done for those deserters, and for us. I think they are going to come back different," Mary added.

I thanked Mary as she walked off. Mark, who had overheard the last part of our conversation, came up to me.

"You should do more than thank her," he said.

"Why?" I asked.

"You just saw an incredible breakthrough, maybe as big as what we have seen with Adam and his group."

"Please explain."

"That is the first time I have heard Mary affirm leadership, but the fact that it was male leadership is even more impressive. I don't know what happened to her, but she is getting free of something big," Mark surmised.

"Thanks for your insight. I did not realize this was such a big thing, but now that you mention it, I can see it," I responded. "Let's keep this between us. This kind of healing can be a very personal thing."

"I will, but she is not the only one getting healed, or delivered of strongholds, by being used to heal others. I don't think I have seen this depth of joy in anyone before either," Mark stated.

"Tell me about this joy you're seeing. I have been thinking that we were running short of it lately," I said.

"In your position you have not had much time to get deep with people, but I have," Mark continued. "I have never seen so many experiencing one of the greatest of joys: the joy of knowing you're doing what you were created for. They may not be smiling or laughing often, but that is because it is a serious business we're in. Even so, I assure you this is the happiest group I have ever seen."

"Mark, thanks for sharing that. I sometimes can't see the forest for the trees. That is most encouraging to hear."

"Are you ready for a little more encouragement?" Mark asked.

"I'll take all that I can get."

"Our relationships are getting deeper and stronger by the day. I've not seen so many people able to open up with each other and share things that are so deep and personal. This means they are growing in trust with each other, which means we are getting much stronger as a people," Mark finished as he walked off.

I was thinking that this was the best news I'd had in a long time when William came up and said that we were ready for the "mission of the day" briefing.

Mark brought up our mandate to find and destroy the works of the devil and asked how we could avoid attacking the evil horde as it was the biggest target of all. William replied that we were not abandoning this strategy, but this one was so big and powerful that we needed a clear strategy before engaging. We first needed to observe and learn all that we could to find any weaknesses that we could exploit.

William added that we needed to go into the fight with a clear understanding of what a victory against the horde would look like. Did we want to drive them off, scatter them, or free the prisoners and see them restored? We agreed to pray for and seek a clear vision of what we were to accomplish before we attacked.

Then we started out with our usual deployment of watchmen around the group. We also sent a few small teams to find and stay in contact with the evil horde, and to gather in all the stragglers or wounded they could before they were captured.

A few hours later, Michael's team brought some of the wounded and dispersed from his old church back to the group. Michael and his team were noticeably excited by their success. By the end of the day our group had grown by several dozen. Soon we would be double the size of our little band that had entered the valley, and we were growing by more every day.

One night it was almost dark when we found a suitable place to camp on a broad ledge that could only be approached from two paths, making it easy to cover with watchmen. We gathered under the bright moonlight for our evening council. I asked Michael to share about their expeditions and what they had learned:

"There are still many people from our old church that are wounded and scattered about out there," Michael began. "It has been some time since the battle that broke out among us, and they are now so tired and desperate that it seems easy to persuade most to let us help them by bringing them here. But their wounds are deep, and most are in terrible confusion. Interestingly, some had glimpsed the evil horde and discerned that it was the devil's army. When these get fully healed they will likely be able to help us a lot."

"Did you encounter messengers from that evil horde?" Charles asked.

"We saw them, but I don't think they saw us," Michael answered. "They were scouring the valley for the wounded and seemed very efficient at trapping any that they found. It was disheartening to see. It gave us even more impetus to work harder to find the wounded and scattered before they did.

"We also noticed that they seemed to just be interested in the wounded. We saw them avoiding the scattered ones who weren't wounded, but I'm not sure why."

"The wounded are the easy prey for them now," Mark said. "They will come back later for those who are not wounded, but are wandering aimlessly. They will capture them too."

"Should we just focus on the wounded now?" Jen asked, as they all looked to me for an answer.

"Michael, did you try to help any of the unwounded stragglers today?" I asked.

"We were so occupied with the wounded and hiding them from the evil ones until we could get them back here that we just told those who were not wounded about our group and pointed them toward you," Michael answered.

"Those must have been the ones who came to us during the day. I think there were only about a half dozen," William said.

"That's about how many we sent to find you," Michael added.

"It seems that it might be a good strategy to point those not so wounded to the group so that the mission teams can focus on the wounded for now," William said.

I then asked Mary how it had been ministering to the wounded that had been brought in:

"I think we were able to get them stabilized. Having someone serve and provide them with fruit and living water made a big change in them. However, I'm concerned about how selfish most of them are, and how demanding they are of those trying to take care of them. This is especially true of those who are not seriously wounded and could easily take care of their own needs," Mary lamented.

"What would you do about this?" I asked William.

"I would give work to all those who are well enough to do anything and have them start serving the more seriously wounded. For those who are demanding service for things they can do for themselves, I would require them to do those things for themselves," William answered.

"What do you think, Adam?" I asked.

"I agree. The fastest way to get them healed is to have them serve others and get their attention off of themselves. That selfish, entitled attitude was a big part of what caused the destruction of our church. We need to go after that attitude whenever it surfaces like we go after the enemies in this valley," Adam replied, with Michael nodding his assent.

"Mary, do you agree?" I asked.

I do, and we will implement this immediately," she answered. "But what should I do with any that do not comply?"

"What do you think you should do?" I asked.

"I think we should stop serving them and let them go hungry or thirsty until they start taking care of their own needs, if they can."

"What will you do if they become disruptive and start infecting others?" I asked.

When Mary hesitated, Charles spoke up:

"Those who refuse to take care of themselves when they are able, or refuse to do work assigned to them, we must leave behind. We cannot keep them in our group and allow their poison to spread."

"What do you think about that?" I asked Mary.

"I know Charles is right, but I just don't see how we can turn people who are still wounded out alone in this place. They will almost certainly get captured by the enemy, at best."

"Mary, if any become disruptive and refuse to follow the policy, why don't you come and get me to enforce it? Just be sure to explain to them completely what we will be forced to do if they do not comply," William said.

"Thank you for your offer, but I think if this is required I must be the one to carry it out," Mary countered.

"Mary, there may be a good reason for letting William or another senior leader do the removing of any that must be cut loose," Mark offered.

"What reason?" Mary asked.

"For healing the wounded, it could be important for you to be seen as non-threatening as possible," Mark responded.

"That may be a consideration, but I think that I should be the one to do any enforcing in my department if I am to maintain the authority in it that I need to do my job," Mary countered. "I also think discipline and taking some responsibility is crucial for their healing."

"Mark, that is a good point," I added, "but I also think that Mary is right. Mary, you should leave what Mark said as an option, but it is your department and you do what you think is right in this."

"I will, and thank you Mark," Mary concluded before turning to me and asking if there were any Scriptures that supported this policy.

We discussed the exhortation in II Thessalonians 3:10, "if one does not work neither let them eat," and the one from Ephesians 4:28—those who were formerly thieves were required to not only work, but work to have something to provide for others in need. After that we talked about the command to "mark those who cause division." Finally, we discussed how Paul commanded the Corinthians to remove the unrepentant one from the church, but when this led to repentance, that one was to be received back with open arms.

It was good to have the discussion, and everyone seemed to understand and agree with the policy we had decided on. After the council, Mary went back to the wounded and explained the policy to them and to her team members. There were a few questions, but the policy seemed to be understood and accepted by everyone. One of the wounded even said that just having clarity about what was expected of them helped.

None of us were aware at the time of how critical this discussion and the implementation of this policy would be. Within a few days, the wounded and stragglers we had taken in greatly outnumbered the original members in our group. Over the next few weeks there were several major developments that turned what could have been a great stress on us all into a positive that led to momentum.

Michael's team continued to get better and stronger. Their success in recovering the wounded and disconnected stragglers brought so much encouragement to the rest that everyone wanted to go with them. Soon just about everyone rotated duty with them. This was a huge source of energy and vision for the entire fellowship. It also brought a lot of respect and trust for the previous "deserters" so that they were not just honored members of the fellowship, but leaders.

The "deserters" not only had their vision renewed, but broadened. They were now very excited about The Lord and His people, and even in the hardest times they never seemed discouraged. They were also growing daily in their compassion for the wounded and scattered. They were now a major source of vision and faith for the whole group. We could not have accomplished nearly what we did without them.

The next major encouragement was discerning that when the demonic messengers discovered our recovery teams, they fled in terror. Noting this, Michael encouraged his teams to attack these demons every chance they got, and it was not long until they were rarely seen anywhere close to us.

One day a main body of the evil horde drifted into our camp. We had called for a day of rest, and had let our guard down a bit, so most of our people were lounging about and were vulnerable. To everyone's surprise, the evil ones not only failed to take advantage of this and attack us, they fled in terror even though they outnumbered us.

The people mobilized fast and mounted a counterattack. This scattered the evil horde and allowed us to recover many Christians that they had bound and forced into the Evil One's service. This nearly doubled the size of our group again in one day.

I was concerned that this was far too many to take in at one time, but that proved to be an unjustified fear. Nearly all of the original members of our group were now moving in healing and restoration gifts. Not only did they prove ready for this challenge, but they handled it with ease. This caused us to consider that we were ready to take in bigger numbers.

Each evening, we had a leadership council meeting. They were open to anyone to observe, and at the end we asked the observers if they had comments or suggestions. This helped to keep everyone informed, but they also felt engaged and connected to our plans and actions. This seemed especially helpful to the new people to fit in faster.

One of the most strategically important developments that strengthened and enabled us to grow so fast was the emergence of small groups. After the council meeting, small groups began meeting all over the camp. It was in these small groups that the people got to really know each other, and even more healing and ministry took place. A profound bonding was happening with all.

These gatherings became so special that they were soon the highlight of each day. We started keeping the council meetings as short as possible so everyone could go to them. It did not take long to see how essential these were to the strength and constitution of the group as a whole, especially as we were adding so many people so fast.

Mary was the most responsible for the growing healing ministry that nearly everyone was now moving in. She learned that she could speed up the recovery of the wounded by quickly putting them to work and increasing their responsibilities. After the accidental collision with the evil horde and the recovery of so many of their captives, the wounded that were in Mary's care became some of the most zealous in helping to heal those who had been a part of the evil horde. It was like watching a constant miracle to see the wounded becoming healers fast.

Mary finally had to confront an obstinate young man who had refused to help with the work. She first mandated that he not be given anything to eat and drink, but that if he was to eat or drink, he would have to go get it himself. He did this grudgingly, but when he continued to refuse to help with the work and tried to sow discord among the other wounded and staff, she sent him packing. This was challenging for many, especially Mary, but the ultimate result was even more discipline and focus in her team. It would be a long time before anyone tested Mary's authority again.

Mary was like a new person. She was even stronger and more resolute, but it was a different strength and resolve, softened by compassion and sensitivity. She loved what she was doing, and it seemed for the first time that she really liked what she had become. She was a queen with authority, but not harsh or threatening. Few had been able to get close to her before, but now it seemed everyone was drawn to her, and she welcomed it.

"Healing is more infectious than disease," Mary said to the council one night. She was perhaps the best example of this.

Mary was now included with William, Charles, Michael, and me in the senior leadership of the group. Mark had started a prophetic fellowship that included the watchmen, scouts, and others with obvious prophetic gifts. The more attention we gave to this, the more The Lord gave us direction and wisdom through dreams and visions.

As I looked around the circle it was remarkable how close we had all become. "This is family. This is *koinonia*," I thought. We had been getting close as a group, but we could have never gotten this close without this valley, and certainly not as we were growing in numbers so fast.

"We have been working and fighting so hard for so long that I have not even thought about how much further we have to go to get out of this valley," Mark commented one night.

"I'm not sure I want to leave it now," Adam said. "I've never seen so much healing and restoration as in this place. I've never felt so much love for His people, or from His people, as I have here. I think we are becoming all that I have ever dreamed that the church would become. I can't imagine leaving this now."

After a few more such comments, it seemed that everyone was looking for me to comment on this, so I did:

"There seems to be two questions on the table: How much longer will we be here? And do we even want to leave since we are seeing so much fruit?

"I have tried to track our course to know where we are. There have been so many days that we moved laterally that we have not made much progress toward the other end of the valley. However, we've made much more progress in what we must become for the times we will be entering.

"I think we have also secured a part of this valley and made it a refuge for wounded and disoriented sojourners. The enemy seems to avoid getting anywhere close to us now, and the word has gone out that this is like a city of refuge.

"We've also become such a large group that we're moving much slower. Unless something changes our pace, we will be here quite a bit longer.

"I too feel that we are experiencing a bonding that is rarely experienced with people, even God's people. Even so, do not be afraid of losing what we have here when we emerge from this valley. Every place we must go through will work to draw us closer to The King first, and as we get closer to Him we will get even closer to one another.

"This communion is *koinonia* and is a taste of the age to come. We must continue to grow in this. We will go through times that will help us to grow stronger in our unity, and then times that will test it. You are very good at passing the tests, but an even greater challenge will begin tomorrow. For now let's enjoy our reward for being devoted to healing, that by this we ourselves are being healed.

"This *koinonia* is a taste of what heaven is made of. We have experienced it and brought it into a place that hell now dominates. Regardless of what happens from now on, remember this—we can have this anywhere, and it is our calling to take it everywhere. This is a taste of the love that God is.

"We know that everything that God does is tested with fire. Tomorrow a major test will begin. This is not to see if what we have can be destroyed, but rather to purify it. So do not be disturbed by this, but be encouraged that The Lord has valued us enough to discipline us as sons and that we are being led to an even greater glory."

"What is coming tomorrow?" several yelled out.

"Our reward."

CHAPTER EIGHT

THE TEST

"So boss, what's the big test?" William asked.

I looked around at the council and the unusually high number of observers who waited for my answer.

"The group must be split up," I answered.

"Why?" several asked at once.

Jen made the question more specific:

"Do not all fellowships strive for unity and growth without having splits? Why would we want to do such a thing?"

"We're too big for our purpose," I responded.

"Too big? We've finally gotten big enough that our enemies flee when they see us," Michael replied. "We also have an abundance of resources to meet all the needs."

"The bigger we are the more people we can help," Mary added.

"This fellowship is the greatest I have ever experienced. We can't just break up something that is getting better and stronger every day," one of the observers blurted out, with seemingly everyone agreeing.

After a few similar comments I was able to continue:

"You all have very good points. This has been the best time most of us have ever had. The Lord has fashioned us into the greatest example of New Covenant church life that I have witnessed. This was not planned or built by any of us, and I would not ever want to do anything to hinder the work of The Lord in any way, but this was accomplished because we were focused on our mission, not our fellowship. If we lose the focus on our mission, we can lose this fellowship.

"I can't imagine being separated from any of you. We now have a foundation of *koinonia* that is rarely found on the earth. However, *koinonia* is not the purpose of our gathering, but it is the fruit of our gathering. It is the fruit of being committed to a higher purpose. *Koinonia* is dependent on us staying focused on our higher purpose. Our mission is now requiring us to break up into smaller groups."

I paused to let this sink in, but there did not seem to be anyone who agreed with me. In fact, if I had asked at that moment most would have considered that it was time for new leadership. William stepped in to help me, saying that they should at least hear me out. So I continued:

"What we have is special. Such fellowship must always be sought as a high purpose. It must be protected as the treasure that it is. What I'm talking about is not dividing from one another, but multiplying.

"Consider these facts: we are now so big and cumbersome that our forward progress has slowed to a crawl. We have been so slow that we have not made it to any of the battles that have been breaking out in this valley recently. We've helped a lot of people, but lately the numbers we've been able to help have dwindled even though our size would have enabled us to help many more. We are no longer agile enough to respond to the places where we were needed. So, we are now mostly just able to help those who somehow drift into our camp.

"I know that we feel safer because of our great numbers, but we are not. As great as the fellowship is, we are losing our edge. When was the last time we brought down an enemy stronghold? Where is the passion we had to set the captives free? That requires more than just healing those who drift into our camp.

"There is a time for comfort, rest, and focusing on building up one another, but not in midst of such raging battles. Our fellowship was born, and built on, being joined in a common mission, with a common purpose. We must keep building on *koinonia*, but it is the fruit, not the focus of why we are here.

"Our brethren trying to make it through this valley are being destroyed or captured by the enemy. We are here to fight! We are here to fight the enemy in every way we can, and anything that hinders us from doing this is hindering us from our purpose."

After a silence, Michael, who was now one of the senior leaders, spoke up:

"Being a part of this church has been the greatest experience of my life. I would be content to stay as we are for the rest of my life, but I have to concur with what our leader is saying. Our great size was the result of our effectiveness, but now it is hindering our ability to be effective in what we are here for."

"Mark, what do you think about this?" William asked. "Have you, or the company of prophets and intercessors you have gathered, heard anything from The Lord about this?"

"Yes, we have," Mark began. "Some have had dreams and visions of us breaking up into many smaller groups. When we did we became even more effective."

"Why haven't you shared this with us?" Jen asked.

"It represented such a major change that we wanted to be sure that it was from The Lord before we did. I think we may also have been affected by what we did not want to see. Not to share this with you and let you discern its source was a mistake, and I apologize," Mark lamented.

"That was a mistake we hope you don't make again, but let's move on. Please share what you believe the overall message of these dreams and visions has been," William continued.

"What we have been seeing was not the result of division coming to us. The smaller groups all worked together, and at times even rejoined for battle, but they also worked independently at times. We continued to be related to one big group, but we were also many smaller ones. We worked together at times and separately at times."

Then a young lady who was observing spoke up:

"As great as our fellowship has become, I have noticed recently that strife has been increasing. Not on major issues, but a lot of minor things. If disputes about minor issues are becoming common then we are not just losing our edge, but we are also beginning to become frayed as a fellowship. I think that if we do not do what you have said and divide the right way, we will become increasingly vulnerable to the wrong kind of division."

"I can't believe that we're talking about this, but it sounds right," Charles added. "Do you feel that The Lord showed you that we needed to do this?" he added, looking at me.

"I don't want to answer that question just yet," I responded.

"Why not?" Mark asked.

"Because I do not want to cut off this kind of discussion," I replied.

"But if you had just told us up front that The Lord had shown you that we must do this, it would have saved us this time and the potential for division that a discussion like this has," Michael added.

"I do not believe in leading by committee," I said, "and I know I could have just announced what we should do, but I also believe that in the abundance of counselors there is safety. For a leader to say that they have heard from The Lord about a matter can cut off debate. Our bond is strong enough to handle the debate, and if it is not then it is time to find out. I wanted to have everyone share from their heart on such an important issue and to be open to additional wisdom about how to do this. We all see in part and know in part, so no one person has the whole counsel of God. I do know what we are supposed to do, but I am still seeking wisdom about how we do it."

"But you have heard from The Lord that this is something we must do?" Mary inquired.

"Yes. I would never have brought it up if this were not so. This is too big of a directional change for me to throw out like this just because I think it is a good idea," I admitted.

"So your issue now is not what we're supposed to do, but how we do it?" William asked.

"That is correct," I said. "All of us are connected in a way that we will always be connected. But even the strongest and closest families must go their separate ways as they mature and move on to their individual life purposes. They can stay in touch and get together when they can. They may work together too, but not many families have the grace to do that continually. In our work we must all stay connected, as we seek to do with the rest of the body of Christ, but we must also be capable of dividing to go after different purposes when needed.

"If we do this right, breaking up into smaller groups will actually help us go to an even higher relationship with each other. Even if we have separation from some for a time, it is just for a season. In due time most, if not all, of us will be joined again. I expect to be reunited again on the Mountain of The Lord. If we do this right our bond will grow stronger, not weaker. Those that grow weaker we should accept as a call to a different place in His body, but there is ultimately only one body of Christ, and we will always be members in that body."

In the short time that this discussion was going on, it was apparent that the overwhelming reticence that had surfaced at first had changed to at least an openness. I had expected it to be a much more challenging discussion and possibly take days or longer to resolve. I marveled at how fast most seemed to grasp that we may need to break up into smaller, more agile units.

"Before we discuss how to do this, can you share anything else you think you've seen about why we must do this?" Jen asked.

"Yes. First, we must continue to pursue this kind of depth of *koinonia* in all that we have experienced here. We have now experienced something that has ruined us for anything less, and this too is a very important part of our purpose to be the family we're called to be. However, we will be in the greatest danger of losing it if we let it eclipse our devotion to following The King and doing His will. *Koinonia* is the fruit of drawing close to Him and becoming united in His purposes, and its lifeblood comes from that.

"*Koinonia* is so wonderful that it is easy to start worshiping our fellowship more than we do The Lord. Remember that selfishness and self-centeredness are the main enemies we're fighting here. It is easy to put so much attention on our fellowship that we lose sight of our ultimate purpose—to follow The King and to go about destroying the works of the devil just as He did. These are the foundation of our fellowship, and we will lose the fellowship if we lose these.

"The worst thing that can happen to any movement is for it to stop moving. We are now so big and cumbersome that we can hardly move. We must become more flexible and nimble to make it the rest of the way through this valley, much less fight in the last battle. We need to recognize that when we have become too big to be responsive or able to engage in our purpose with the agility needed, it is time to break up into smaller groups that can."

"This resonates with me," Charles offered to a surprisingly large chorus of 'amens.' "So what are some of your ideas about how to do it?" he continued.

"The first question is: should we divide into two groups or more?" I began. "After that the question is how do we determine who goes with each group?"

"If The Lord spoke to you that this is something that we must do, did He not tell you how to do it?" one of the observers asked.

"No. He did not," I replied.

"Why does He give us clear and specific directions for some things, and then for things as important as this He does not?" Jen asked.

"When you read The Book of Acts you see this too," Mark answered. "Sometimes He's very specific, and at other times He seems to leave working out the details to His people. Obviously there are times when He wants us to go through the process of working out as much as we can, when we can, so that we grow in wisdom and the knowledge of His ways.

"The Lord does not just give us guidance, but He wants to be our Guide. He does not just give us instructions, but works with us as we pursue Him. He sent us The Helper, not The Doer, so He will not do the work for us, but He will add to us what we are lacking. It is a good thing when He trusts us to work things such as this out as it indicates He considers us mature enough to do this."

"Since you have obviously been thinking about this longer than we have, do you have some thoughts about how we should do this that you can share now?" William asked me.

"Yes," I began. "One of the things that has made this group so effective is how each one found their own purpose and were given the opportunity to do it. To help heal the wounded, we got them engaged as soon as possible in serving others, and their wounds healed faster. As long as we have been engaged in doing what we have been called to do, we have had little bitterness or jealousy to deal with. This has enabled us to get as large as we have without fracturing, but rather growing even stronger in our unity. It was only when we got so big that we were not able to get to the wounded and scattered to serve that all of the small disputes began among us. That should be a barometer to us.

"We now must split up into the unit size that best serves our purpose here, and we need to repeatedly divide as needed to keep them the right size. However, I don't think it is a matter of one size fitting all. Some groups may need to be larger or smaller than others according to their purpose, or even because of the places they are being sent to.

"We also need to keep a balance of ministries within the groups. Each new group formed needs to be a composite of all of the diverse ministries and gifts that have been growing here. Our diversity has also been a great strength.

"We also need to stay in contact with each other, seeing each other as a part of the same tribe if you will. We must be able to respond quickly to come to the aid and support of one another, and continue an interchange that will be helpful to each group. If one group becomes overstaffed with one ministry and another has needs in that area, these can be shared. Likewise, if one group encounters an enemy too strong for them, they can call for others to come to their aid.

"For this reason, the continued contact and communication between all of us will be very important. Again, we must keep in mind that we are not dividing from one another, but rather multiplying to become more responsive and effective, but we must remain one family, or tribe."

I paused here for feedback. It was positive and insightful. The main questions were how we would decide who went in each new group, and who the leaders of each one would be. When I was asked which group I would lead, I felt that I should respond with another part to the plan, even though I had not expected to get nearly this far in our first meeting about it and was wondering if I was sharing too much at one time. I underestimated them—they grasped everything even faster than I had been able to.

"I think William and I should not lead a group, but rather be devoted to keeping all of the groups in contact with each other. By us staying in communication and being able to visit groups where needed, we can connect those who have needs with those that have resources that can help meet those needs," I offered.

After some comments about this, the general plan as outlined seemed good to everyone. Someone recommended that those who were gifted at multi-tasking also be assigned to William and me for support so that we could stay focused on keeping the groups interconnected and related. We also determined to have a general council meeting at least once a week with representatives from all the groups, along with any observers who desired to attend.

I had expected a long, ongoing debate, and probably many challenges that could take days to resolve, if not weeks. Instead we had a plan and agreement about it, all done in one short sitting. The immediate dread of breaking up into smaller groups had been turned into a vision that everyone seemed to share. I could hardly believe it. I had greatly underestimated the people, and The Lord who knows how to prepare them for His purposes.

Some still had questions, but since we already had a lot to do to implement the plan, it was recommended that they record and pray about an answer for their question. They could then present these to the council with a possible solution. If they could not find an answer in a reasonable time they should bring it to the council as just a question. This at least had everyone seeking to address every challenge by seeking a solution for them.

It was not just me—all seemed to be aware that what unfolded in this council was a work of The Spirit. He had spoken through many different people. As this meeting ended, many smaller groups walked off in animated conversation.

Mark, Mary, Jen, William, Michael, Adam, Charles, and I were soon left standing alone.

"This was no less a miracle than anything else we have seen," William began. "I have been in many serious, high level strategy meetings in my life, but I have never seen anything like what we witnessed here tonight."

"I have never been in a serious, high level strategy meeting before," Michael said. "In our old group, such a gathering would have been inconceivable, but I know I was a witness to the miracle here tonight. This openness and interchange in a serious decision making meeting is so encouraging. I can see why you do it this way."

"Why is that?" I asked.

"You steered them, but you did not dictate. In this way you allowed them to have ownership in the plan. You could have dictated what we should do, but the way you allowed this to unfold it is now their plan too, not just yours. This gives everyone much more reason to ensure that it succeeds," Michael elaborated.

"That is good insight," I replied. "I think this is a fruit of having these kinds of open councils. However, getting people to buy in was not a conscious intent. I encourage this kind of input because I know very well that we all see in part and know in part. I wanted to be open to others seeing parts to this that I did not yet have. But that is a good insight about how this does help people to feel a part."

"I feel trust and confidence in the direction we're going. I also know that for you to have the faith in us to hold a meeting as open as this one, you have great confidence in your own leadership," Michael said, looking at me.

"It may seem that way, but I think every day I have less confidence in my own leadership. I am not saying this to be humble, but as a statement of fact. I'm in way over my head, and I know it more each day. I am comfortable in this job only to the degree that I keep my trust in The Lord to be our Head, and to guide us.

"I have also grown in my trust in all of you, and a respect for your perspective and wisdom. So I want to hear it, but I am especially seeking to hear The Lord speaking through different ones as I know He likes to do. The Lord likes to speak through less known and less appreciated members of the body, so I want to ensure that they can be heard as well. But as much as I have come to love and trust all of you, I trust The Lord even more. I am not seeking to hear you as much as His voice through whomever He chooses to speak."

"I really am starting to get this, but aren't you concerned that arguments and even division can break out?" Michael asked.

"I am actually more afraid of disputes or arguments not breaking out. They are usually the result of people caring enough to contend for what they believe. The more passionate the defenses, the more I know they are committed.

"Now if this group was immature, or we had not grown in our bond through all that we've been through together, as well as the great things we have seen, I would be concerned about such disputes. I'm confident now that we are not only mature and strong enough for them, but that they can be healthy. I only want to see the disputes kept civil and above personal attacks. We must be mature enough and strong enough to handle disagreements or we will not last long in this world that is descending into such chaos.

"That being said, even if our arguments about this matter had escalated to the point of us dividing acrimoniously, I knew that it was so important to break up into smaller groups that even if it happened that way, it would be better than where we were headed if we did not do this."

"So you would have even let this erupt into a church split in order to attain the ultimate need of breaking up into smaller groups?" Mary demanded.

"That was in no way my desire, but if cells in our body do not divide when it is time, but rather just keep on growing and consuming the resources of the body without regard to the rest of the body, they have become cancerous. Then they become a bigger threat to the whole body.

"Cancer is ultimate selfishness on the part of individual cells or organs. That is the main thing we are fighting in this valley. When it is time for separation to happen, to delay it can be the most dangerous thing we can do. So if it is not done in the right way, it must still be done if even in a less than perfect way," I explained.

"Think about Paul and Barnabas. Because they did not separate the right way it happened in a less desirable way, but it had to happen. It was time for them to go in different directions. Paul learned this lesson well and was after this quick to send out those who were ready to expand the ministry."

"I know this is the right thing for us to do now, and we could not have waited much longer without putting the whole group in jeopardy," Jen added. "We were becoming self-focused, and there was a growing pride in what we had that was not good. It is so hard to grow and mature in what we are called to be and do without becoming prideful. Did you see this happening? Is this why you brought it up tonight?" she asked.

"I did see it, but did not bring it up tonight because of that," I responded. "I had an agreement with The Lord that He would be our Shepherd, and so I sought Him about what to do, how to do it, and when to do it. I was then able to witness Him building us into what He wanted us to be. I am not the head of this group, He is. It is my job to follow Him.

"If this were a device of mine I would not have much confidence going forward, and honestly I would have been afraid to split the group up. I am going forward with great confidence now having watched Him do through all of you what He did. We are not called to be just a strong force, but a force that is a family—His family. Tonight we had a family meeting, with the Head of the family presiding. He did this through the different members of the body. I know that He alone could have done what we witnessed tonight, so I have great confidence going forward."

The next few days were spent working out the practical details of the plan. It did not go perfectly. There were disputes, challenges, and more than a few hurt feelings. That is life, and this was a good indication to me of how much life there was in our group. Even so, the senior leaders spent some time mediating and praying for those who felt offended or rejected, but hardly as much as we expected.

Ultimately we broke up into a dozen groups, the number that allowed each one to be staffed adequately for the journey. The "headquarters" staff had grown to include messengers designated to keep every group in touch with the headquarters. Others with administrative skills were given to us to keep up with the positions of each group on a map, along with details about their strengths and needs.

There was another map that laid out the position where battles were unfolding, or positions where the enemy was expected. Each new group was given a different stronghold to attack or battle to engage in. As soon as these began to move out, we knew that the strength of our whole plan would soon be tested. We did not have to wait long as it seemed that the gates of hell were immediately opened for every kind of attack on us.

As the attacks came it quickly became apparent that the strategy of multiplying in smaller groups was far more critical for us to meet this challenge than we could have foreseen. It is not likely that we would have survived this in our previous state, and it was apparent that a new level of warfare had begun.

CHAPTER NINE

THE BATTLE

After we had broken up into the smaller groups, the speed of our advance picked up quickly. We felt like we were a force again, and we were. We were looking for the enemy with a resolve to fight, and we were looking to save and restore the wounded and scattered.

As we moved we came in contact with an increasing number of groups that were also moving through the valley. We began to see common denominators in the groups that were successfully navigating the valley, as well as with those that the valley was defeating.

The successful ones were those that had taken seriously the mandate to attack the enemy strongholds at every opportunity. This not only kept the enemy on his heels and less able to attack them, but more importantly, it kept them with an edge and focus that was hard for the enemy to attack—from within or without. This also gave little opportunity for petty relational conflicts to arise that keep groups more inward focused than outward.

The groups that became self-focused inevitably fell to the main spirit of the valley: selfishness and self-centeredness.

There was no doubt this is where we were headed before we separated into smaller groups. This was a sobering and continuous reminder of what a powerful enemy we faced that could cause so many to become more self-centered than Christ-centered.

As I passed through our camp, I marveled at how mature and strong everyone seemed. This valley was transforming us much faster than any other experience I'd had going through this valley. I think it was doing more in me this time. I knew it was the *koinonia*. As is written in I John 1:7, "**If we abide in the light as He Himself is in the light, we have fellowship** (Greek *koinonia*) **and the blood of Jesus His Son cleanses us from all sin.**" It is also written that "the life is in the blood," and His life flows when we are rightly connected to His body in true *koinonia*. This cannot help but to result in growth and maturity in The Lord.

The first time I went through the valley I felt that I had been made into a capable warrior, but this time I was being made into a warrior-healer, as we all were. It was great to see the enemy flee, but it was even better to set his captives free and see them healed and restored.

So fighting and healing was a wonderful combination that worked to form amazing character. It was a combination of fierce resolution tempered by compassion. In my experience, we tend to see one or the other in a person, but it is rare to see both. Here you could not make it far without both, and both were being equally developed in us.

Every day we expected to encounter the main force of the evil horde, or at least an enemy stronghold, and we usually did. Then we went for many days where we saw nothing of either. What we did find were multitudes of wounded from groups that had been devastated and scattered. From these we added large numbers to our group each day. Our healing ministries had become so effective that most recovered and were restored fast and added to our scout, watchman, and healing teams.

By this time it was expected that everyone had a primary job or ministry, and they knew their place and functioned in it. Everyone was also able to work in other types of teams when needed. We each developed the specialties that we were best at, but we learned skills in just about everything. So everyone was employed and engaged every day. Because of this, there was not much time or opportunity for the rumors and divisiveness that plague most churches and movements.

As long as we kept moving and occupied it seemed that all went well. Just as water must keep flowing to stay pure, people do too. People must have vision, purpose, and a destination. Israel celebrates the Feast of Unleavened Bread to remember that they had to leave Egypt in such haste that their bread did not have time to become leavened. Leaven speaks of two things in Scripture—sin and wickedness, and legalism. We might say lawlessness and legalism. Either of these will creep into our lives if we stop moving and growing in The Lord.

We also kept adding more groups to keep the numbers manageable in each one. Even so, the twelve large groups ultimately grew to fifty, all of which were still larger than the initial twelve. Many thought that this must be the harvest that Jesus said would be the end of the age, but it was just the preparation for it. There was a lot of preparation needed just to oversee such a great number being gathered. We did not always do well at preparing these groups as some would go out on expeditions and be lost to the valley.

This led to a dilemma. If we took the time to prepare the people better, we would not have time to gather as many of the wounded and scattered and restore them. We prayed constantly for the right balance. Every time a group or groups would be lost, we would trend toward equipping and training.

Then we would realize we were not helping recover nearly as many as we could have. It seemed that we were constantly turning the dial to more training, or to more gathering, and finally resolved this would be constant as conditions changed.

William and I decided to each take half of the groups so we could give them better oversight. Soon we needed even more help. We added Charles and Mark to the senior oversight team, and then soon after that Michael and Adam. That was still not enough because we were adding people so fast. Then we found an unexpected source of effective leaders.

We had recovered a few of the leaders from groups that had been decimated. As soon as they were healed enough, we taught them our basic leadership principles, mostly about discipleship and fast delegation of authority. We were surprised how fast many of these were willing to learn such a different style of leadership. We did the same with them that we expected them to do for others, delegating and adding them as fast as we could to our leadership. It worked out much better than we had hoped. To our surprise there was almost no reverting back to authoritarian or centralized control by these retooled leaders.

Still, the whole assembly of those under our general oversight was growing so fast that it was getting far beyond our ability to lead, and we knew it. We accepted that we were just there to give general direction, and to help direct the repositioning of groups and resources to meet opportunities and needs. There was a great unseen hand on everything, and we mostly just marveled at the extraordinary work that was being accomplished to reap such a big harvest.

However, this was a harvest of fallen, wounded, or disoriented believers, not new converts to the faith. The Great Commission was to make disciples, not just converts, and most of these had been made converts, not disciples. We were making them into disciples, but we looked forward to the time when we would be leading brand new believers to The Lord and seeing them become disciples.

Even so, there was great satisfaction in seeing many who had been atrophied in their walk being taught, trained, equipped, and then engaged in the ministry they were called to. As big as we had become, and as fast as we were growing, everyone still got to know their place—the job they were called to do and how to do it. We were not just a mob, but rather an increasingly effective force.

Even though we had visible human leadership, we all sought to follow The Lord and be used by The Holy Spirit. The main thing He did to build the strength and cohesion of the entire movement that we had become was to especially anoint the small groups. They had become the heartbeat of the whole force. As the life and vitality of the small groups grew, their basic form or pattern changed and then they became even more so.

When the small group movement began, each one had an emphasis, such as healing, teaching, prayer, growing in the gifts of The Spirit, etc. As these groups matured they became general gatherings where everyone would bring something to the meetings according to the biblical exhortation Paul gave to the Corinthians. One might bring a short teaching, another a song, another a testimony, a prayer, a word of knowledge, etc. Because of this, every meeting was unique and could go in any direction that The Spirit led. This made them much more organic and powerful. Everyone came to them with the expectation of watching The Spirit do something marvelous, and rarely was anyone disappointed.

This also required the leadership of the small group meetings to change. The best overseers became those who were the most sensitive to letting The Holy Spirit lead. Given this place, The Holy Spirit would move in the most fascinating and brilliant ways. More often than not, there would be a harmony in the overall message and flow of the meeting that was so extraordinary that we recognized no human hand could have done this. Those who left these meetings knew they had been in the presence of The Lord and had learned greatly about His ways.

In this way each gathering became something where virtually everyone who came would know that The Holy Spirit had spoken directly to them, taught them, healed them, or touched them in some way. These meetings became more about meeting with The Holy Spirit than meeting with other people. This caused the *koinonia* to grow. There is no bonding between people like there is when you experience The Lord together, or when He uses you to touch someone else. As stated, this all worked to bring us to the place where the main source of the power and life of the entire movement was the small groups.

The power and life in the small groups had become so well known throughout the valley that no one wanted to be in a movement or large group that did not have them. This had obviously been orchestrated by The Lord because they would be essential for the ultimate harvest that we were all being prepared for, as well as for the last great battle. Strategically and tactically, we had to learn how to take in large numbers, but also ensure that they were taught, trained, equipped, and then engaged in their purpose as fast as possible.

I could not help but to marvel at how the little group we had entered the valley with had become such a multitude. We all knew that this was not our doing. The Lord had built this, and He would have to lead it as well. We were in way over our heads. This was not like running a large corporation, or even an army. We needed miracles every day, and we continually needed wisdom that exceeded the combined wisdom of all of us. We were so aware of this that our main devotion each day was simply to seek His instructions and carry them out. The Lord was The Captain of the host, and He was the only one who could be The Captain.

So the senior leadership spent most of their time in prayer, going about and teaching. Some of the gatherings for teachings were large and might take the place of the small groups for a week or two when the senior leader was doing them on an important and timely subject. Even so, no one wanted to miss the small groups for long as they truly were the lifeblood of the movement.

All of this contributed to a daily life that had become so exciting and edifying that we had stopped being concerned about when we would make it to the end of the valley. The presence of The Lord working in our midst was so great that virtually all leaders at any level were fearful of putting their own name on any part of it. It was all The Lord's and we were just laborers in His field.

After experiencing The Lord's leadership like this, any human leader looked pale and weak in comparison. Presumption in leadership stood out as so incongruous that it became very rare. Any who became possessive of a part of the work, or self-seeking or self-promoting, would stand out and would be humbled so quickly that this also became rare. The presence of The Lord had grown so great that anything but leadership that was based on following Him just did not work.

When we started to encounter other groups, they had evolved in essentially the same way. There were unique strengths and weaknesses in each one, as well as some unique characteristics. Even so, as we met with the leaders of some of these groups, I had the impression that we could have exchanged leadership with any of them and no one in either movement would have noticed much of a difference.

The most common belief that we all had about leadership was that this whole thing was beyond us, was not our doing, and we were mostly just along for the ride it seemed. This is not to imply that most did not have significant strengths and knowledge, and all could be proactive and decisive in what they were shown to do. That being said, all had a healthy understanding that the ultimate leadership was beyond our ability. This was indescribably encouraging to the real leaders. Trust in Him gave the rest and peace in what otherwise would have been a burden far too great for any person to carry.

As big and powerful as we had become, there were still attacks from without, and they began to increase. As strong as we had become in our unity, there were also some divisions that rose up from within. I had always wondered how Aaron, Miriam, and the other rebels in the camp of Israel had been so arrogant as to rebel against Moses with The Lord so present among them, but as an old friend used to teach, and what I now know is an irrefutable truth: "People Are Crazy!" All of us are insane to the degree that we are not abiding in The Lord, and we can drift very far from Him in our hearts even while in His presence. This we learned.

Some of these attacks and divisions were devastating and left many wounded. However, because of the way the body was now functioning they did not stay wounded for long. The healing ministry had become so effective that all wounds were healed fast. The only ones that were not healed were those that got separated from the group. These would usually get picked off by the enemy fast.

Those that became separated and picked off by the enemy were the ones that were not quick to forgive, or were easily offended. They could be very strong, wise, and mature in every other way, but these two things would make them vulnerable. As we learned, this forgiveness and the resolve not to be offended were messages shared repeatedly throughout the camps. We also learned to watch out for any who were succumbing to offense, or were not forgiving quick enough.

As we moved, we won battles. Some were significant. We suffered losses with every battle. It was not just the size of the battle that determined the losses as we suffered some of the greatest losses in some of the smaller battles. We learned that the threat was not about how big the enemy was as much as what the enemy was. The enemies that were the most effective against us were criticism, accusation, and self-righteousness, though at times great losses came from greed and lust. These seemed feeble in comparison to some of the other enemies we faced, but they wreaked great havoc among us.

The enemy also seemed to be getting more effective at finding unhealed wounds to sow his poison into. This is where many of the divisions within the camps came from. Because of this, even the smallest unhealed wound became a very serious matter. The further we got into the valley, the more dangerous any unhealed offenses or wounds could be.

Over time the nature of the accusations being hurled at the movements in the valley became increasingly extreme. We did not pay much attention to these at first because it seemed that they were getting so extreme that no thinking person would take them seriously. That proved to be a big mistake as there were not as many 'thinking' people as we supposed. For a long time the enemy had worked at changing education into indoctrination, especially in the mentality of the Accuser. It was paying off for him.

Everyone who was not in a tight group that watched out for each other was beginning to suffer almost constant wounding, and people started to react more to pain than to

reason. The effect of the constant accusations and rumors was that the people were quickly conditioned to accept them.

It then began to feel like the very atmosphere of the valley was being saturated by a terrible and toxic flammable gas. We began to sense that even a little spark could set off a massive persecution. It was not long before the spark came.

A factor that had made us vulnerable to what unfolded was how our successes had caused us to become contemptuous of the evil horde. We were almost daily recovering our brethren who had been captured by it because it was so easy to raid. We did not even suspect that this was setting us up for the enemy's biggest weapon of all—pride.

As our contempt for the evil horde grew, our vigilance gradually decreased. For this reason it became easier for the enemy to raid us and to surround us with every evil power. Then they began to get inside the camp. The Lord warned us over and over through dreams, visions, and the watchmen, but we had become so comfortable and arrogant that we could not hear the warnings, or even see the signs that we were vulnerable.

When the onslaught began, we were fighting in every direction from without and within, and against a fury we had not experienced before. The results were immediate and devastating, then they got worse. In just a few days our conversation had gone from how to totally defeat the enemy horde to wondering if any of us would survive.

The casualties from friendly fire were soon as great as those from the evil ones. Large groups started breaking away from the main body and disappeared into the valley. Some of these

reappeared to viciously attack us. We were soon down to half our recent numbers, and losing more by the day.

We looked for help to come from the other movements in the valley, but none did. Later we found out that every other advancing movement in the valley was also being attacked with such force they could not come to our aid. Neither could we go to theirs. We had been caught in a perfect storm. Our arrogance had weakened us and blinded us to the enemy's strengthening.

As should have been foreseen, the most destructive attack on us came from accusations. Most were outlandish, even incomprehensible, but when they came from other movements in the valley and were fueled by the atmosphere of jealousy and distrust that had been subtly building, we were trapped in a diabolical crossfire.

Most of the petty innuendo we had refused to answer, or even acknowledge. This turned out to be a mistake. We learned the hard way why the New Testament epistles were filled with the apostles countering such attacks—they would prevail if they were not confronted. Even though this understanding came late, it did help when we began to counter the assaults.

When we began to push back on the assaults, not by attacking those making them, but sometimes just simply stating that they were not true, it began to turn the tide. We had been so used to being on the offensive we hardly knew how to fight defensively, but when we did take a stand on anything it helped, and sometimes could stop a huge onslaught.

As we began to stand and recover some of our aggressiveness, the results were quick and dramatic. This restored hope, and hope is a powerful weapon in any battle. Faster than we could have imagined, the tide turned. The storm died down almost as fast as it had broken upon us.

By this time there were very few of us left. We had lost more than 90% of our numbers. Everyone who was left was wounded, and some badly. We did not know it at the time, but the evil horde had just about completely expended itself in the attack. Our pushback, as feeble as it seemed, had not just been a shock to the evil horde, it exposed how weak it was. Quickly the enemy camp was dealing with their own divisions and rebellions.

After just a few days of relative rest, we were recovered enough to begin sending teams to raid the enemy camp. We were determined to recover as many of ours that had been captured as fast as we could. We were so successful that the enemy moved as far from us as they could.

We then went into pursuit mode, but were too weary to go far. Even so, the word that we were on the attack again brought back to us some of those who had been scattered. The healing ministries that had been so effective before went to a new level. We were now only a fraction of the size we had been, but we were becoming a force again. We were also wiser and far more humble.

With the enemy now at such a distance, and those in our camp so exhausted, we decided to take a few more days to rest and evaluate all that we had learned. We started with the victories we had achieved against the enemy strongholds. We looked at what had worked and what had not worked. The lessons were profound. We could not help but to think how much more effective we could have been if we had known much of this when we entered the valley. So, we recorded our conclusions to distribute to others in the valley.

The healing teams did the same for the most effective ways to dress and heal different types of wounds. We also gave an account of how the spirit of accusation had been used to set us up for the most deadly attacks, and how our arrogance had opened us up to what had nearly destroyed us. We held nothing back, even our most foolish and embarrassing mistakes. We also told about how our hope had been recovered, which resulted in our ultimate victory.

That is, if the conclusion of all that had happened was a victory. To have lost so many hardly felt like a victory. But we had survived, and not only survived, we got back on the offensive, driving the enemy off and starting to recover and restore the wounded and scattered.

Because our reputation had been so assaulted, we questioned who might want to read these accounts, but we trusted that they would be helpful to at least some who might come into the valley. We felt a great anointing writing them, and thought that these lessons were far too valuable not to pass on if possible.

The enemy horde had been populated mostly by captured, deceived Christians. The horde called itself "the true church" and was recognized by most non-Christians as the real church. We were "outside the camp," and most of the groups like us that were fighting through the valley were now considered cults or sects that were in rebellion to the church.

Even though we were now a fraction of what we had once been, we could not help but to be encouraged by the way our people had fought. We were small now, but we were still strong enough that the evil horde that outnumbered us many times over had retreated after our relatively weak counterattacks. This gave us more reason for hope.

We could not help but to be concerned about what this battle had done to all of the bystanders in the valley. To them, this great battle was considered to have been a great civil war in the church. We wondered if we had so muddied the water that it would have a major impact on the coming harvest in that part of the valley.

As we surveyed the potential of those that were left in our camp, I considered that we could be an even more powerful force than we had been with our great numbers. They fought well when it seemed unlikely that any of us would survive. But we had survived, and even turned the tide again. Our faith level was now higher than ever because of it.

At the height of our pride we actually considered our pride to be faith, but now we knew that there was a big difference. It was not likely that we would make this mistake again. Knowing this as we did now could make the biggest difference going forward.

As our wounds healed, our *koinonia* fellowship went to a new level as well. Few things bond people together the way fighting in and surviving great battles can. We had been welded together by an ultimate adversity and survived. It was a unity greater than we had experienced, and unity unleashes even more faith and power.

We did not know it at the time, but this was what The Lord was after far more than the great numbers we had been able to gather. He cares about numbers and desires for all to be saved, but this unity was going to be much more important for the battle to come and could result in the salvation of many times more.

So we were a far smaller group, but we felt that we were a far more powerful force now. Even so, the enemy had done a masterful job of wounding almost everyone in the valley and creating increasingly acrimonious divisions between almost every group passing through the valley, and also among the races, cultures, and other identities of non-Christians living there.

These divisions were fed and increased by agents that sowed self-pity everywhere. This seemed a ridiculous strategy of the enemy, but it turned out to be one of the more brilliant ones.

This produced a victim mentality in almost every group that kept them far away from the things that could have healed their wounds. Everyone was hurt, mad, and quick to blame others for their pain. This was setting the whole valley up for violence like there had never been before. But that would also be a set up for a healing ministry like the valley had never seen and one that all of the great battles had been used to raise up and prepare.

As we began to move forward again, we were appalled by how the great battle had left so many wounded scattered all over the valley. There had been multitudes of devastated churches, movements, and missions. We set about to recover and restore as many as possible, as we had learned to do, but it seemed now to be many times more daunting of a task than before.

As our numbers and strength were being replenished, we started to consider how to go after the evil horde again to recover all who had been lost. We did not know that this would not be necessary. The weapons that the enemy had fashioned to use against us would be the source of the demise of this part of his army.

The evil horde was considered to be the true church now by most of the wounded people in the valley. With such poison flowing through them, the people began to accuse the evil horde for their problems. With the atmosphere so charged with bitterness and rage, the extreme accusations made against the horde rose very fast, and soon even eclipsed what had been hurled at us. Then different groups within the horde started blaming and turning on the others in their company. The meltdown and devastation came fast, and was so complete that we just stood and marveled.

A result of this was that the multitude of Christian captives were freed, but still very wounded, oppressed, and bound in spirit. We then tried to move as close to the battle as we could to help recover those that could be healed. Some could, but some were so wounded from this catastrophe that they were much more outraged and toxic than those we had met the first night in the valley. We were able to help a few, but only a few.

Soon we had no choice but to move out of the region of devastation from the evil horde. Powerful spirits of fear were moving in to gather the horde again into an army bound together by fear. Soon the evil horde was bigger than before, and growing. There was nothing Christian about it any longer—it was a religion, and a very dark one.

We had no choice but to back off. The entire valley was now inflamed and far more dangerous than when we had entered it. The groups and movements like ours that had been considered cults and sects were believed by most to have been eradicated. However, those that were left were doing what we were doing—seeking to understand the situation we were now in and seeking The Lord for what we should do. We knew that we were still here to destroy the works of the devil, but now those works had seemingly become much stronger and many times more numerous.

In council we resolved to continue following the path, staying close to the living water and recovering and restoring those that we could. We would continue to attack every stronghold of the enemy we encountered, just as we had been instructed.

We had just begun to move when we came to the gate.

CHAPTER TEN

THE TABLE

We stood in front of the gate. It appeared to be brass and not very attractive. We could see the path behind it for a short distance, but in the fading light of the evening we could not see very far. As we looked around we saw the beginning of other paths leading in different directions. Since it was almost dark, and there was a nice clearing nearby, we decided to camp for the night and determine which path to take in the morning.

The leadership gathered together for the evening council meeting. Those who wanted to observe gathered around too, as was our custom. I began by recounting some of what we had just been through in the valley. We had fought hard, and I thought we had fought well. We attacked every enemy and every evil stronghold that we encountered. We had many victories, but our successes had led to a pride and carelessness that set us up for a terrible and costly defeat. To a large degree we had recovered as a group, but our mandate had been to leave the valley in better shape, and we all felt that there was little doubt that we left it in far worse shape than it was when we entered it. But, we were still in the valley, so there was yet time to turn this around.

"How had so many great victories not resulted in the valley being better, not worse, for our having been here?" Jen exclaimed. "It seemed that we were on the verge of driving the enemy completely from the valley, and then in one major onslaught we lost virtually all that we had gained. The valley is now in more turmoil than ever. A little pride was the leaven that set us up for that," she lamented.

For a long time no one had anything to say. Finally I spoke:

"We can't judge too much by appearances. We paid a dear price for our pride. It let us slip into the delusion that we had attained a place of peace and safety just before we were almost destroyed," I began. "The positive could be true as well. It may look bad now, but we may have helped set the stage for others to take back the ground that we lost and learn from our lessons so that it is not lost again.

"That being said, I think there is one other thing that we failed in that could have resulted in leaving the valley in much better shape now. That is if we had been more devoted to building than just fighting. We should have built more fortresses of truth—secure bases where sound teaching and some of the great healing ministries that we've seen developed would be available to all. They would be places of refuge that are more permanent for serving the weary and wounded sojourners passing through."

After we discussed this for a time, and everyone seemed to agree with it, Adam changed the subject:

"So, what do we do now?"

"We must fight on," Mark declared. "Those were our instructions. Until we are told to stop, or do something else, we have been made into warriors and that is what we do. I agree that we should be builders too, but our main job is to fight."

"What do you think we should do now?" I asked Michael.

"I think we should go back to where we last saw the evil horde, track it down, attack it, and recover our brothers and sisters that are still captives in it," he began. "We are far more effective as fighters, and we've learned a crucial lesson about the deception of pride. I don't think we will be vulnerable to that again, and I think we must go and fight for those we lost."

I marveled how one who had just recently been known as a "deserter" could now be so loyal to those who had in many cases deserted us in the great battle. As I looked around I could tell many others were thinking the same thing.

"Michael, I think you are called to do just that. I think you should take all who feel this call and do just what you said," I replied.

"But what about you? Won't you be coming with us?" someone asked.

"No. I've got to go through that gate," I said.

"Why?" another asked. "There are many paths that lead from this place. Why would you take the one with the gate?"

"I've seen this gate before," I began. "In a dream, or a vision, I can't remember, but I know I have to go through it. My destiny is wherever the path behind it leads."

"Will you take the rest of the group with you?" William asked.

"I will take any who feel that they are supposed to go with me, but we have come to a place where many paths diverge. We have come to this place at this time for a reason. I think some of us are called to take each one, and only a very small group is supposed to go with me through the gate," I answered.

"But we are already such a small group, compared to what we were, and we are now so strong together," another interjected.

"We are," I answered. "However, there is such strong leadership in all of you that you now need to build and lead your own groups."

"But we've been leading, and some here have led very large groups," Mary protested.

"True, and you've been remarkable, but you've been under William and me. You don't need us anymore. You know The Lord's voice, and you know how to stay close to Him. There are many who need you to lead them now, and you are ready."

This was a word no one seemed to like, but all seemed to know it was true. We had been a band of misfits and discontents, but walking this path together had caused us to become closer to each other than we had ever thought we could with anyone. Just thinking about parting from one another was excruciating, but we knew this was not a time to follow our desires. The highest purposes of The Lord had to be our first devotion. This now required many of us to take separate paths.

"I think the paths that go from here will lead some of you back to where we began to walk this path," I continued. "You are going to find waiting for you those whom you have been prepared to lead through the valley.

"There is one thing we must do before we split up," I added. "Tomorrow you must all follow me for just a little way down the path beyond the gate."

"Why?" Mary asked.

"There is something that we must experience together. I'm sorry that I cannot tell you more, but I do not know more. However, this is something we must do together tomorrow."

Everyone agreed that they would go with me on the path beyond the gate to experience whatever it was. Most seemed to think that it would be a meeting with Elijah and/or Enoch. I also thought this might be the case, but I knew that it was crucial for us to experience whatever it was before we went any further.

As we moved toward the gate the next morning, we all had many questions about our experience in the valley. I was hoping for a good debriefing to help us better understand all that we had been through. We had just been through some of the best experiences, and the worst, in our lives. Even so, it seemed that everyone was ready for more as we came to the gate. As I looked at their faces full of expectation, I was nearly overwhelmed with how thankful I was for such fellow sojourners on the path.

There was no lock, or even a latch, on the gate—it just swung open as we pulled on it. We entered and started down the path. The path was wide and beautiful, but narrowed as we went until we could only go single file. Then it opened up all at once into a stunningly brilliant and colorful clearing. As we entered it we were amazed to see gorgeous tables with beautiful white linen tablecloths set with the provisions for a great feast. There was a host that I did not recognize and many servers to welcome us, which they did with great joy.

The servers seemed to know everyone, and directed each one to a special seat prepared just for them. I went up to the host and presented myself as the leader of the group.

"Welcome," the host said, smiling broadly. "We are honored to have you here."

"Do you know us?" I asked

"I do," he said as he directed me to one of the tables.

I was given a seat next to the head of the table, which he took after everyone had been seated. The servers began filling our cups with a brilliant wine that had the same sparkle as the living water. When I tasted it, there was nothing I could compare it to. It had the rejuvenating affect of the living water, but even more so. The only way that I could describe the taste was that it was perfect.

We sat in quiet awe as plates were then served to each of us. To everyone's surprise they were all different as they were our individual favorites. Many of us had been daydreaming of just such a dinner as we had been eating only fruit for so long. It was like they had seen our daydreams and were now making them come true.

As I looked around, it was a glorious scene. No one had ever witnessed a more beautiful, captivating, and welcoming setting. We had been so focused on the tables, our host, and the servers that when we began to look at the perfect carpet of grass and the canopy of beautiful trees, it caused a whole new level of wonder. Could such a place exist in the midst of the valley that had been so threatening?

Our host gave thanks and we began to eat and drink. It took a bit for the conversation to get going, but soon it was a great and very animated celebration.

"You obviously know us very well," I said to the host. "This could not be more perfect."

"The King takes care of His servants," the server replied, who was leaning over my shoulder and placing a glass of the living water next to the wine.

As I looked up at the server, I realized that they were angelic and not human. Then I looked at our host and knew immediately that this was The Lord. He just looked at me smiling. I did not know what to say, or how to act, so it took some time before I could speak. Finally, I did:

"Lord, I'm sorry I did not recognize You. I'm sorry that I did not offer a proper protocol," I muttered as I started to get up so I could kneel next to my seat. He stopped me.

"I appreciate your intent, but we are here to honor you and what you have accomplished" He said, speaking of the group.

I looked around because the increasing clamor around the tables had subsided fast as others noticed that those serving them were angels, and some had begun to suspect who our Host was. He then stood up, and everyone's attention was riveted on Him. Some started to move from their chairs to the ground, but He told them to remain seated. No one said anything. A few had begun to softly weep. The Lord continued:

"Be at peace and enjoy. As you have noticed, your servers are My messengers and your personal angels. These were created to minister to the heirs of salvation, and these have served you your whole life. Serving you is their great joy. They know you better than you know yourselves. They are not here just to serve you, but so that you can get to know them better. You will need to know them better for what you are entering.

"I also have something to say to each of you, so I will spend a little time with each of you. First you must enjoy this feast that we have longed to have with you."

The King then sat down and began to eat and drink with obvious joy. We did the same. The conversation was slow to start again, but after a few minutes it was as animated as before. As I looked around I did not know if I could contain the joy as I wondered how anything could be better than this.

"This has to be a part of heaven, and right in the Valley of the Shadow of Death," I remarked to The Lord. "'Thank You' is not adequate."

"This is a piece of heaven, and it is right in the middle of all of our enemies, and all of the death and evil. If you can experience heaven here, you can experience it anywhere. Now that you have made it to this table you are welcome at My table anytime," He replied.

"Lord, this is a truly wonderful place, but what really makes this heaven is that You are here, and these angels," I said. "The living water and the fruit have been more than wonderful, and I have never tasted anything as wonderful as this food, but it is being with You, Your presence, that makes this heaven."

"True," He replied. "But I am with you everywhere, and so are the angels. That is what you are on the path to learn. It is more difficult to see Me with you everywhere than it is to see Me here like this, but as you grow you will see Me everywhere, because I am with you everywhere. I will never leave or forsake you. Your journey is to know Me as I Am. I have been as close to you every step on the path as I am with you now. To see Me is to walk in truth."

I had never felt so awkward as I did trying to eat with The King sitting right in front of me. I had been visited by The Lord before, and had experiences before His throne, but never in such an intimate and casual setting as this. He was more regal than I could describe, but He was at the same time as casual and approachable as a carpenter. I wanted to focus on His "carpenter side" so I could relax, but decided that I wanted to experience Him as He was, so I would just have to force myself to relax. As if He knew my thoughts, He reached over and touched me on the shoulder and smiled in a way that put me at ease. Then He told me to ask Him anything I wanted.

"Lord, I would like for this moment to never end," I began. "I'm sure all of these feel the same way. Yet, obviously this will end and we will have to continue our journey. I certainly do not want to divert from anything You want to say to us during this time, but I would like to ask You some questions about the journey.

"Lord, You said that this was to celebrate what we had accomplished in the valley, and to honor us for it. I know You would only speak the truth, but it seems to me that we left the valley in worse shape than when we entered it. Please tell us what we accomplished," I asked.

"First, as you were told in the beginning, a main purpose of this valley is to help fashion My people into what I have called them to be. I am pleased with what this has done in you, and in those who are with you," He said looking around at everyone. "Do you, or any of those with you, think that if given another opportunity to go through the same experiences, you could do much better?" He asked.

All at our table nodded that we could as He continued:

"Of course you could, and you will have many opportunities to use what you have learned and what you have become.

"Next, you think you left the valley in worse shape because of how it seems the darkness has spread and captured many more people. It appears that way, but let me share with you another perspective—My perspective.

"The darkness did not spread or multiply as it may seem—it was there all the time. You just exposed it. No one who was truly serving Me was captured by the evil horde. It only captured those who did not seek Me first, but rather sought their own interests. Those are the only ones that evil can take dominion over. It was such that created this evil horde, and such have fed its growth.

"This evil has been able to dominate much of the world that is built on the ways of the Evil One. Just because they used My name does not mean they follow Me or serve Me. You helped to expose many for what they have always been.

"Some will come to their senses as the nature of this evil horde becomes increasingly obvious. These will turn to Me and repent of their own evil ways. They will be free and will help many others to be free. Many of these are even now considering both the real nature of what they are now in, and what has become known to many of how you fought back, freed others, and have remained on the path.

"A purpose that I gave you was to attack the strongholds of the Evil One to make it easier for those who would come after you. You did this. Though much of the world now thinks that My church is being destroyed, My church was only strengthened by what has happened. My church has always been a remnant—mostly hidden ones within the multitudes who have claimed to serve Me.

"You think that because you lost so many people to that evil horde that you lost My people who were in your care. I am My people's Shepherd, and I have never lost a single one. I had many people in that evil horde that are now free because their eyes were opened to what it truly was—another Tower of Babel. Men have built many things using My name, but they were really building to make names for themselves. Many continue to have the folly of thinking that they can reach heaven by their own wisdom and strength, like the first tower in Babel.

"Again, even those with you that were captured that were My people are not lost. They are being educated and set free from their own self-seeking. They are scattered all over the valley, but right now they are beginning to discover the materials you published about your experiences. Those materials will help them to be ready to join the movements that are about to move through the valley. These here at this feast will soon lead many of them, and they have been prepared well for this.

"So, we do have much to celebrate. Many laborers for the greatest harvest of all have been prepared. How can we not celebrate?"

The Lord looked around, seemingly engaging each one as they were all looking at Him. We were greatly encouraged by His assessment of what we had done in the valley. Then He turned to me again and asked:

"You must sit with Me where I am seated to see things as they really are. This too you will learn to do, but what do you think about what I just said?" The Lord asked with a smile.

"It is more than encouraging. You really do work all things for good for Your people. I know our mistakes, such as letting our pride set us up for such an attack, were still mistakes. However, it is so wonderful to know that even that will work out for good.

"There is no way that we will ever be able to thank You for letting us be a part of Your purposes, to serve You like this. It has been more difficult than any life I could have imagined, but also far better and fulfilling. Just today has been worth all the years of struggle many times over. To know that we did accomplish something good is like icing on the cake."

"I chose you for this job because you are perfect for the job," He answered. "I made you, and I prepared you. One reason I chose you is revealed by your question—you care about those I put in your care, and you do your best to do a good job with everything I give you to do. You must be more at peace about your inadequacies. They will be the areas of your greatest strength when you learn to rest more in Me, trust Me more.

"Your shame over your failures are like anchors holding you back. I paid the price for your failures and your sins. If you have repented and still feel shame, this means that you really do not think My sacrifice was enough to pay for them. When you fail to rest in Me and what I have done for you as you should, you begin to move in your own strength. That will wear you out and weaken you so that sin is able to afflict you. It is hard to have good judgment when you're tired. This was the correction I gave to you years ago when you were close to burn out, and you are still wrestling with it."

I remembered the incident well. I was in my office feeling that I could not take any more pressure from all of my responsibilities. Then The Lord came into my office. I did not see Him, but I didn't need to because His presence was so real. All He said was, "I uphold the universe with My power. I can help you with this little ministry." The experience only lasted about a minute, but the refreshment I received from His presence was so great that I immediately felt I needed another world to save; this one was too easy!

"Lord, I'm sorry. I keep falling into the same trap," I responded.

"You do, but be encouraged. You're making progress," He replied. "You would not have made it this far if you had not. You not only made it this far, but you brought all of these with you. You have much left to do. I don't want you to fall short of your full purpose. The main enemy of your full purpose is the deception that would have you put more faith in your inadequacies than in My ability. If you believe in Me you will rest in Me.

"What do you think is your greatest strength as a leader, and also your greatest weakness?" He asked.

This question surprised me. I had to think about it for a minute before answering:

"I think the greatest strength I have is that I am bold and decisive, but I also think I have made enough mistakes in life to be humble about it and correctable when I know it is from You.

"I think my greatest weakness is that I do not spend enough time in prayer and just sitting before You, listening to You. I think that is also related to what You just said, my failure to rest and be at peace in You, to know You as my strength and salvation."

"I agree with your assessment," He replied. "What would be the main thing you would like Me to do for you for your journey?"

"I would like for the fullness of The Holy Spirit to be released in this group so that together we have all of the gifts of The Spirit, ministries, and the fruit of The Spirit, to fully manifest You in every place."

"Why this?" He asked.

"Everything we need is in the gifts and fruit of The Spirit You gave us as The Helper. I can't think of anything else that we would need other than what He is to us," I answered.

"You have answered well, and you will have what you asked for. Is there a special gift of The Spirit that you would like to have manifested in your own life in greater measure?"

"The gift of a word of wisdom," I replied.

"Why that gift?" He asked.

"Well, it seems to be the most important thing for any leader if Solomon, the wisest man, would ask for it. If all of the gifts are released in those who are with me, I will need the wisdom to help apply them to the events and situations on this journey," I answered.

"You will have it," He said.

"Lord, may I ask one more thing?"

"Yes."

"May I join You as You speak to each of these?"

"Yes, you may, but why do you want to do that?"

When the all-knowing God asks us a question, He is obviously not seeking information; rather, He is trying to get us to see or consider something. So, I took a moment to really determine why I wanted to do this.

"I don't know how I could learn more about these people, or You, than by watching how You speak and relate to them like this," I answered.

"Go and get Mark, Andrew, Charles, Jen, and the two Marys, as well as Adam and Michael. I will speak to them first, and then I want all of these to be with us as I speak to the others."

"How perfect are His ways," I thought as I went to get the others. My next question would have been to ask if they could join us as He spoke to the others. This was the greatest experience of my life, and it was about to get even better.

As I went to get those He had called for, I looked over to where the path led on from the clearing, and there stood Elijah and Enoch. They were both smiling broadly, obviously enjoying the whole scene. It seemed fitting for them to get to do this.

There was no Host like The Lord. I could not imagine a more special scene in all of creation like Him hosting His people in this place. I could have stayed there forever, but I knew that the two prophets stood where they were to prepare us for the next part of the journey. I thought of the conflict raging all over the valley, and I looked around at this part of heaven we were standing in. He said we could take it with us, that we could join Him at His table anytime, even in the midst of our enemies as we were now. This we must determine to do.

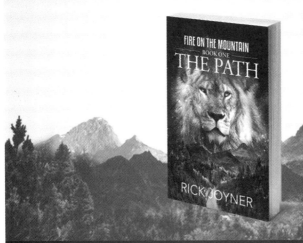

MorningStar
PARTNERS

Our MorningStar Partners have grown into an extraordinary global fellowship of men and women who are committed to seeing The Great Commission fulfilled in our times. Join us in equipping the body of Christ through conferences, schools, media, and publications.

We are committed to multiplying the impact of the resources entrusted to us. Your regular contribution of any amount—whether it's once a month or once a year—will make a difference!

In His Service,

PARTNER WITH US TODAY

MSTARPARTNERS.ORG
1-844-JOIN-MSP